BEANY AND THE BECKONING ROAD

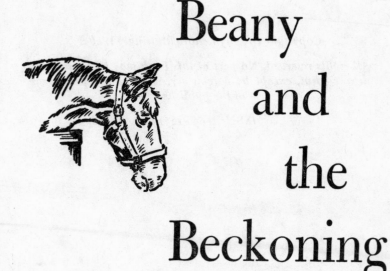

Beany
and
the
Beckoning
Road

by Lenora Mattingly Weber

THOMAS Y. CROWELL COMPANY, NEW YORK

MANUFACTURED IN THE UNITED STATES OF AMERICA
PUBLISHED IN CANADA BY FITZHENRY & WHITESIDE LIMITED, TORONTO

To

ELIZABETH RILEY

Who Understands How
the Road Can Beckon Home

Contents

BEANY AND THE BECKONING ROAD

1

The day was perfect for painting lawn furniture. The sun was hot and the riffling breeze was helpful in drying paint as well as keeping designing mosquitoes off the tanned expanse of Beany Malone left uncovered by her blue denim shorts and halter of red bandanna.

When Beany had announced that morning that she was turning into an *ex*terior decorator for the day, her nineteen-year-old sister, Mary Fred, had said, "But not in that Southern Riviera outfit, I trust. Here, slide yourself into the Malone painting costume," and reached in the closet for a whacked-off pair of Levis and a paint-streaked shirt which had once belonged to their brother, Johnny.

Beany had muttered, "I don't have to look like Huckleberry Finn just because I'm painting."

Mary Fred had stared at her a surprised moment before her ready laugh bubbled out. "You mean you don't

have to look like Huckleberry Finn when Norbett
Rhodes, cub reporter on our rival paper, has his vacation
the same time you have yours and, being on the loose, just
might show up?"

Beany's answer was a guilty flush that momentarily
dimmed the marching formation of freckles across her
nose and cheeks.

It was the first of July and the first day of Beany's two
weeks' vacation from her summer job. This gathering together the lawn furniture and painting it was something
her housewifely fingers had itched to do ever since she
had read an article in a magazine about the fun of outdoor
supper parties.

In the shady protection of their big chestnut tree Beany
carried or dragged all the unmatching pieces—slanting-
backed wooden chairs, straight-backed metal ones, the
heavy table with its top warped by sun and rain. Some
were a weathered red, some a chipped and flaking white.
But a coat of apple-green enamel would "tie them together" as the magazine article, with its pictures and
recipes, promised. "Eye appeal, appetite appeal."

Once Beany, going around the roomy, sprawled-out
house for a deck chair, paused beside a rosebush which
was like a bouquet of bright pink. Gentle memory
brushed Beany. Her mother, dead now for six years, had
planted it. Beany remembered how she, a little girl of
eight, had stood beside her and asked, "What kind of a
bush is it?" And her mother, looking up from her patting in of damp soil around it, had answered, "A rosebush, honey—a Three Sisters' rose."

The younger Beany had turned that over in her mind.

"You mean an Elizabeth and Mary Fred and Beany rose?"

"That's right," her mother said, laughing. Why, her laugh, Beany realized as she stood there in the hot sun, was like Mary Fred's. . . . Another picture tugged at Beany's memory. Her father's saying that chill November day when they returned from the cemetery, "We'll all have to mother each other now. . . ."

Beany sighed. She had often envied girls whose fathers were the always-at-home variety. Martie Malone was the leading columnist on the *Morning Call* and was frequently away from home, sending back stories to the paper. "Our off-again, on-again, gone-again father," Johnny Malone always called him. And yet, Beany comforted herself now, even in his absence they all felt a warm togetherness. They could always count on his interest, his understanding.

The apple-green enamel obligingly covered blisters and blemishes. Ah, this was fun! Beany stroked paint on the arms of a chair. The arms were wide enough to hold a plate, provided its owner kept a wary eye on it. Her brush strokes kept time to her humming. For she could picture Norbett Rhodes lounging in this very chair and saying, "Peppermint-stick ice cream! All this and heaven, too." A tear-sized globule of paint trickled onto one of the charms of her charm bracelet. Norbett had given her the charm bracelet for Christmas, had shopped for the charms that were significant to *them*. He had asked her never to take it off. "The charmed charm bracelet," Mary Fred called it. Beany meticulously wiped off the paint with a corner of her paint rag, painted on.

And it was nice to be free of the troubles of troubled

people. For Beany's summer job was helping Eve Baxter
help people. Every day letters poured in to the Eve Baxter
column on the *Morning Call* from persons in distress who
asked for counsel or help. Beany sorted the letters, typed
the answers Eve Baxter dictated. Both the letters and
answers were read by thousands over their morning
coffee.

But now it was Beany's vacation. "Have yourself a fling,
young'un," Eve Baxter had said in her blunt way. "Do
you good to get away from the woes of the world. You
bruise too easy."

It was true. Sixteen-year-old Beany couldn't be just a
typist. Her soft heart ached right along with the mother
of three who wrote in, lamenting that her husband never
gave her either a dollar or a kind word. Or with the sick
and senile man, none of whose seven children wanted
him in their homes. Eve Baxter had constantly to restrain
Beany from opening her purse strings, her heart, or the
Malone home to those in grief or need.

The noon sun rose higher in the sky and Beany, stopping a moment to flex her tired right arm, glanced at the
big, gray stone house. She hoped her brother Johnny
would remember to fix something for lunch. "Get along
with your painting, little Beaver," he had promised, "and
I'll call you when lunch is served."

But Johnny was reading about an old pioneer by name
of Jim Bridger, and Johnny was apt to lose himself so
completely in old-timers of the past and their cooking of
buffalo meat over a fire that he forgot that the Malones
of the present could do with iced tea and sandwiches.

Now only the glider was left unpainted. Its faded,

lumpy, and torn cushions were to be replaced by some Beany had seen one noontime in a downtown store. Deep maroon with a sea-horse design in crisp white and this apple green. Beany did a little mental arithmetic. Out of her money earned as typist, she had already bought the charcoal burner over which hamburgers or wienies would sizzle. But she had thirty-eight dollars left. That would buy the new cushions *and* a matching umbrella as a final country club note. They'd have a lawn-furniture warming on the Fourth of July. When she saw Norbett they'd talk over whom they'd ask.

She wished Norbett would come. She longed to show off her handiwork, to hear him say, "Well, ain't you the one!" which was his way of saying, "Beany, you're wonderful." And wouldn't a swim in the park lake be cooling and restful after this hot, arm-tiring job! The paint would be drying all the while they swam, all the while they lay on the beach and planned their Fourth of July party.

The noon sun had shortened the shade of the chestnut tree. Beany set down her paint bucket and brush. She tugged and pulled at the unwieldy glider to get it out of the scorching sun.

Suddenly the noontime quiet was shattered. A little boy in cowboy boots with an overgrown pup at his heels came dashing around the grape arbor, brandishing a toy pistol and making a noise like a bleating goat—though it was supposed to represent a machine gun. The bucket, a third full of paint, was kicked over. Beany exclaimed, "Oh, Martie—I could boil you in oil! Now I'll have to buy new paint to finish this glider. And I was hurrying to get it done so if—"

She didn't finish the sentence. Even to a small nephew of almost five you didn't blurt out that you hoped Norbett would come whisking up the driveway in his red car and ask you to go swimming.

She dropped on her knees, hoping to salvage some of the paint. The brush, handle and all, was covered with it. A horsefly took that second to light on Beany's chin and, though she tried to swat it with her wrist, she smudged her chin and cheek with green paint.

Martie, the culprit, backed off looking like a contrite, fair-haired angel. Not so the half-grown pup, Mike, who loved the world and saw no reason why the world shouldn't love him back. He cavorted through the spilled paint. Then, in a rush of affection, he leaped upon her, transferring some of it from his sticky paws to her blue shorts.

An exasperated Beany fought him off, put the sticky paint bucket and stickier brush out of reach, and went through the house and up the stairs to Johnny's room. "You promised to keep Martie and Mike inside till I finished painting," she accused him.

Johnny was sitting at his typewriter desk in the middle of an array of old letters, journals. He lifted absorbed black eyes to Beany's irate blue ones. His tall, lank figure left the swivel chair with a bounce as he looked about bewilderedly. "Well, gee, I gave him a blanket to make a tent out of—and I thought he'd stay put. I was just reading about old Jim Bridger getting lost in a blizzard. Say, maybe this stuff I use to clean typewriter keys will take the paint off your face—"

"It's my shorts I'm worried about," Beany said, somewhat mollified. No one could remain irate at Johnny long.

She stood while Johnny daubed and rubbed at the blue denim, while he took careful swipes at her chin and cheeks. "There you are, precious, smelling like ether, but immaculate."

"I've got to go up to the boulevard to get some more paint. Johnny, I'm starved."

"That makes it unanimous. Get your paint and I'll have a luncheon ready for you such as you never ate before. Is our Mary Fred back from the dentist's yet?"

"She will be any time."

Beany set out for the paint store on the boulevard. Only to meet disappointment. The paint store was sold out on that particular shade of green paint. Here was forest green, or turquoise green—

Beany walked home in the hot sun empty-handed. Oh dear, now she must shop all over town for the right shade of green to tie her lawn furniture together. And she had planned that everything should be perfectly dry and usable for the Fourth of July three days off. Her planning enthusiasm dropped a notch or two.

She turned down her own Barberry Street, tired and hot. She passed the white-pillared colonial house of Mrs. Adams, the Malones' neighbor on the south. Beany paused a moment at seeing a car with the door of its baggage compartment yawning wide. Mrs. Adams' housekeeper was helping to load in a hatbox, a folded car robe, and a thermos jug. The Malones called their neighbor Mrs. Socially-Prominent Adams because her name constantly appeared in the society column. Ordinarily Mrs.

Adams had a benign, yet superior, aloofness but this hot
early afternoon, she turned a beaming face toward Beany
and said, "Oh, Beany, isn't going on a trip fun? I'm going
to Yellowstone Park."

It was at that very dissatisfied moment that Beany felt
her first tug of longing to *go* someplace. Somehow, even
painting lawn furniture lost its glamor. She thought ruefully, Going places gives everyone a certain shine.

She thought of Kay Maffley, her school chum, and of
the morning she and Beany had said good-by. Kay and
her mother were leaving Denver and returning to Utah,
where Kay's father worked. Kay had grieved at parting
from Beany, and from Johnny who had dated her a few
times. But when the time came for stowing assorted luggage into their cream-colored roadster, Kay's face was
all sparkle and excitement. "Mother says we can make
sixty on that road through Wyoming."

Beany reached their gate and here again was the frolick-
ing Mike. Red, their Irish setter, walked toward her in the
slow dignity of mature doghood, his red plume of tail
wagging his welcome; he looked askance at Mike's ca-
vortings in a disgusted way that said, "Isn't that fellow
ever going to grow up?"

Beany patted Red's nuzzling head with one hand, with
the other she pushed away Mike. Red's brownish-red coat
was exactly the color of Norbett Rhodes's hair, through
which he was always nervously running a comb. . . .
Norbett *knew* this was the first day of her vacation. Involuntarily her eyes glanced up the street. . . .

But there was only the mailman, who greeted her and
handed her a sheaf of bright-colored post cards. Some

were addressed to Johnny, some to Mary Fred. Three were
for Beany Malone.

Vacationers—traveling vacationers. She longed suddenly to be the one sending the post cards, not the one
standing here in her own all-too-familiar front yard reading them. She turned over the one which showed a red and
orange sunset over a Utah peak. That would be from Kay.
The message read, "We are spending a week here. Warren—remember the boy I wrote you about?—drove
Mother and me up. Having a wonderful time."

Absence certainly makes the heart grow fonder for
somebody else! If ever, Beany recalled ruefully, any girl
worked to get her brother to date her girl chum she,
Beany Malone, had. And now Kay's letters, Kay's post
cards were full of someone named Warren, who was a
wonderful dancer, wonderful swimmer, said the funniest
things, *and* had a blue convertible. But then, Beany realized honestly, Johnny wasn't grieving either. Johnny was
absorbed in Jim Bridger, hardy pioneer who had been
the first to discover Yellowstone Park.

The next card was from Beany's cousin, Sheila, who had
lived with the Malones this past school year. Sheila, too,
had taken a trip back to visit her professor uncle and her
card, too, said, "Having a heavenly time." The heavenly
time, Beany knew, was because a certain brash and
freckle-faced student was attending summer school
nearby.

The other picture post card to Beany showed a rodeo
scene. On it was scrawled in a man's heavy writing, "Still
wandering the world through searching for my lost
Quaker." It was signed, "Your roving cowboy, Ander."

Beany smiled. Ander Erhart wasn't *hers;* he was Mary Fred's. And he wasn't a *roving* cowboy, though he had been a cowboy until he left his family's Wyoming ranch and came to attend medical school and live with his aunt next door—the same Mrs. Socially-Prominent Adams whose car had already gone streaking down the street toward Yellowstone Park. Ander was just being nice to her, Beany, because she was Mary Fred's sister.

And Beany knew—dear knows she'd heard enough talk about Quaker!—that Quaker was a roping horse which Ander had owned and trained, and then sold when he went into the army. But now Ander, as well as a sympathetic Mary Fred, was combing the country for the roan Quaker, because Ander planned to enter some rodeos in California and towns along the West coast. "With my roping arm and Quaker under me," Ander had said, "I could win enough prize money to put me through another year of pre-med."

Beany turned the bright, alluring post cards over in her hand. Everybody going places, seeing things. Everyone but Beany Malone. What good was a vacation if you kept right on sleeping in your same bed, eating the same old meals that you had to cook or help cook yourself, after first lugging the groceries home from the store?

Standing there in the hot sun Beany looked discontentedly at the Malone home.

There were three large, two-story houses in this block on Barberry Street. Mrs. Socially-Prominent Adams' occupied a spacious corner at one end. On the other side of the Malones' was the Judge Buell residence. The judge's son, Carlton, who was Johnny Malone's chum, had beat a path across the otherwise immaculate lawn to the Malone side door.

Funny, Beany mused, how houses take on the personality of their owners. Mrs. Adams' white colonial with ruffled curtains at every gleaming window, with flower boxes adding a color note which was repeated in the awnings, was like Mrs. Adams, herself, tastefully dressed for one of her parties with hat, veil, gloves, and jewelry matching.

And the Judge Buell residence with its massive front door, its drawn draperies, was like the judge—dignified, judicial.

Beany's eyes rested on the roomy Malone home. Its windows were opened wide, its screen door bulged from dogs impatient to get in or out, its front steps were scuffed. The house looked as casual and hospitable as Johnny sounded when he called out, "Come in—come in! Never mind cleaning your feet—what's a little mud in our lives?"

Then suddenly Beany's heart registered a bright red car turning onto Barberry Street. Let Byron or Keats, or whoever it was, write about a heart lifting up when he beheld a rainbow in the sky. With Beany it was,

> *My heart leaps up when I behold*
> *A red car in the street—*

Yes, it *was* Norbett. He slid up to the curb with his usual flash and flourish, stopped with his usual scrunch of brakes, greeted her with his usual offhand, "Hi, gal!" He came toward her with that nervous, impatient walk which Mary Fred had once called, "Norbett's strut." His thin, tense face had an absent smile. "What're you leaning against the fence post and looking pensive about?"

"Post cards from travelers," Beany confessed. "Everybody's going places—"

"Having a wonderful time. Wish you were here. X marks the spot where we went swimming," Norbett finished glibly. "Beany, is your father home?"

"No, he's still away, covering the probe at the state penitentiary. We're hoping he'll get home today."

Norbett didn't answer. There were several different Norbetts as Beany had discovered in their often stormy going-together. The heart-warming Norbett who said nice things and lifted her to the clouds. That was the Norbett who had given her the charm bracelet and asked her always to wear it. The show-off Norbett who talked about his newspaper job and called politicians, or the celebrities he interviewed by their first names. There was the moody, trigger-edge Norbett— Oh, but she didn't want him difficult and touchy today!

She began talking fast, hoping to make him into the Norbett she was happiest with. "Guess what I've been slaving away on! Painting the lawn furniture to match— and I used part of my money for a charcoal burner so we can have supper parties outside. This magazine article I read said that food had a special flavor when you sat in the twilight with the sun sinking and the food sizzled over glowing charcoal—"

She paused, waiting for Norbett to say, "Well, ain't you the one!" which would mean, "Beany, you're wonderful!" If he said it, then everything would fall happily into place, and she wouldn't feel this restless, left-at-home discontent. She wouldn't even mind if she couldn't match the green for the glider.

But Norbett said, "—and the mosquitoes humming merrily."

She went on, "and this article gave a lot of recipes. There's one for bean-hole beans, and you dig a hole and put in the beans and salt pork the night before—and I thought we could have a supper party for the Fourth of July and watch the fireworks at the stadium from our yard—"

"The Fourth?" he interrupted. His eyes didn't meet hers. "Don't count on me, Beany. Might be I'd be busy on an assignment—I mean a story."

"But it's your vacation, Norbett," she said, feeling a chill letdown.

Someone was calling and Beany looked up to see Mary Fred coming down the street. "Any mail for me?" Mary Fred wanted to know.

Norbett said, "Why hello, Mary Fred. I thought you were up at a ranch in the mountains wrangling horses for dudes from the East."

"I am—I mean I was," Mary Fred said absently, riffling through the cards. "I left town the day after college exams were over, but I pulled a filling out of a tooth on a piece of taffy, and they gave me a few days off to come down and have it filled." She put her hand to her cheek and grimaced. "The excavating is over. I'm famished. Has lunch been served at the Malone snack bar yet, Beany?"

"Johnny said he'd fix something."

"We can always hope. Oh, here's word from Ander—"

Mary Fred's voice dropped two notches in disappoint-ment. "He hasn't found Quaker yet. Not a word from any-one, though I ran ads in our *Morning Call* and in *your* old *Tribune*, Norbett."

"*My Tribune!*" Norbett gave a grunting laugh. "Look, gal, I'm just a pencil sharpener down there."

"But you're a reporter," Beany defended.

"Just of the D.A.R. meetings, or some old lady celebrat-ing her hundredth birthday. Never a nice, juicy mur-der."

Mary Fred said, "I wonder if I ran a big, boxed ad about Quaker if people would notice it more—"

Beany said quickly, "Let's go in and see what Johnny's up to. Come on, Norbett." They must not let Mary Fred get started on the missing Quaker with the Lazy E brand on his left hip (or maybe right) and his two white feet (or maybe three).

Mary Fred *was* diverted, "I can't eat anything chewy. Get away, Mike—I've got on stockings."

The three entered the dim and cool front hall. Above their heads came a warning, "Sh-h, turn the volume lower." It was Johnny, who was treading softly down the stairs. "Ah, deary me!" he sighed, impersonating an anx-ious housewife, "I've been rocking and singing to little Martie for half an hour. I hope my luncheon dish isn't ruined."

Beany was the first one to reach the kitchen at the end of the hall. On the stove their biggest kettle bubbled merrily. She bent over it and sniffed. She never remem-bered smelling exactly that smell before. "What's this you're cooking, Johnny?"

"That, my pet, is I-haven't-the-slightest-idea."

"You haven't the slightest idea? Well, you know what you put in it, don't you?"

"Not the slightest idea," Johnny insisted. He picked up a long, wooden spoon and stirred it, and turned to smile at his two sisters and Norbett Rhodes.

"Behold the smile," Mary Fred said. "The dentist, with whom I have just spent some burning moments, said he'd be willing to pay Johnny to sit in his waiting room and smile. Just as an advertisement for perfect teeth."

But Johnny's smile did more than reveal a flash of perfect teeth. It had a rare quality that drew everyone within its radius into an intimate, even exciting rapport.

Beany reached for the spoon to taste the mixture, but Johnny held up his hand. "Wait, little Beaver! There'll be no tasting until we dish it up. I was sitting up in my room reading about old Jim Bridger, one of our early-day trail blazers, in case you don't know—"

"As though we could live in the same house with you and not know it," Beany murmured.

Johnny had graduated from Harkness High in June and was already enrolled at the university. Because he had made a study of early-day history, had even helped compile a book on the history of their state, the folklore professor of the university had asked his help in preparing material on the old scout who had built Fort Bridger.

"I didn't know Jim put out a cookbook of his favorite recipes," Mary Fred said.

Johnny gave her a withering look and went on, "I was reading about the old boy being lost in a blizzard. He had to hole up in a bear cave for a day and a night—"

"With the bear?" Norbett wanted to know.

"No, the bear leased it to him for the nonce. And when the blizzard let up he set out for home, plowing through snowdrifts with the sun glaring down on the white expanse—"

"I never saw such a mixture," Beany interrupted, lifting up a spoonful. Tomatoes evidently gave it the coral color. There were kernels of corn in it, pinkish-white crescents of shrimp.

"Go on, Johnny," encouraged Norbett. "We got to get old Jim Bridger home."

"By the time he reached his dugout he was so blinded by the snow he couldn't see. Just light from dark. And he was weak with hunger—and so, by gosh, was I as I sat there reading about it! So he fumbled through his cupboard. They had a few canned things in those days—milk, tomatoes, beans; the bullwhackers used to gamble for the chunk of pork in the beans. Anyway my ravenous Jim found five different somethings on the shelf and dumped them in a pot together. And he said he came up with the most heavenly stew, the like of which he had never eaten before or after. So I came down and pretended I was snow blinded and took down five cans—"

"Just imagine," Mary Fred said. "We are about to dip into a stew with canned dog food, pumpkin, sauerkraut, and, no doubt, a can of scouring powder for thickening."

"Johnny Malone," Beany said, "you surely didn't come down here and pick out five cans of stuff without *looking* at them?"

"Is there any law against it?" Johnny defended. "I put a

blindfold on so I wouldn't follow any preconceived ideas. I groped my way to the can opener on the wall and opened them. I even put the empty cans in a sack so I wouldn't know. But while I had the blindfold on, I stepped on Martie's foot, so I had to take time out to solace him and get him to sleep."

Norbett laughed with hearty enjoyment. "Johnny, I wish you'd hurry up and get famous. If I was your press agent, I could turn out wonderful stories about that genius, Johnny Malone."

"Here, let's dish up the I-haven't-the-slightest-idea," Mary Fred said, reaching for bowls in the cupboard.

They sat down to it at the round kitchen table in the roomy Malone kitchen. Almost simultaneously each blew on the first spoonful to cool it, and then tasted it gingerly.

Norbett said, "Why, it's not bad. In fact, it's swell."

Mary Fred said, "Allowing for the filling in my tooth which gives everything a slight dental-laboratory flavor, it has that certain indefinable something."

Beany studied hard her second spoonful. Tomatoes, shrimp, corn, perhaps a can of chicken and noodle soup —but there was another flavor that she couldn't define. A piquant, nutlike flavor. "Johnny, I wish I knew what was in the fifth can or jar. Can't I look at them?"

"No, my sweet. That'll be something for you to think about when you lie awake at night."

"Fancy a Malone lying awake at night," Mary Fred said.

With that, Red, who was lying in the middle of the floor where everyone must walk around him, leaped up with a wild whimper of delight and streaked into the hall.

Such an expression of ecstasy could mean only one thing. That the front door had been opened by the father of the Malones, their off-again, on-again, gone-again Martie Malone.

2

"MY HEART DROPS DOWN—"

There was one question the Malone children always asked their father even as they welcomed him. They asked it over the bustle of kissing and handshaking and making room for his chair at the table, "How long are you going to be home, Father?"

The man who had Johnny's slender height, Johnny's dark hair peppered with gray, Johnny's warm smile a little tempered by years, and a myriad of laugh wrinkles around his eyes, answered, "Just till tomorrow. I had a chance to get a ride down and I thought I'd better look in on the Malone orphans. But," he added hastily, "this probe at the pen won't last much longer, I hope. Then I'll be back on your hands for a while."

Martie Malone was more than a columnist on the *Morning Call*. He was an altruist, a crusader, a fighter. His typewritten column was always championing a cause.

For ten days he had been sending back unbiased news stories on the investigation of prison conditions. Martie Malone's column, even as Eve Baxter's, was read by the whole city. "You can always depend on Malone to give you the true picture," readers said.

Johnny hurried to set before him a bowl of his I-haven't-the-slightest-idea and explain about its inspiration. Mary Fred told him about the ill-fated piece of taffy which had necessitated her leaving the ranch resort and coming to the city for a few days. "It's back to my horses and dudes tomorrow or the next day. You have to gentle the horses, and toughen the dudes—and I love it," she ended.

Beany made iced tea, which they carried with them into the living room. "Let's go into the living room and live," Johnny always said.

Above the clink of ice and the stirring in of sugar, Beany heard a small step on the stairs. She said, "Oh, Norbett, hold my glass a minute," and made as hasty a dash toward them as did Mike, the too exuberant.

She reached the sleepy-eyed little boy and swooped him up in her arms. Not that little Martie wasn't perfectly able to come down the stairs alone; it was just that his young legs could not stand the overwhelming onslaught of Mike. He said thoughtfully, "Johnny put a can of corn in his soup, didn't he, Aunt Beany?"

For some reason young Martie always put "aunt" in front of Beany and Mary Fred, but never an "uncle" in front of Johnny's name.

Beany's curiosity prompted her to ask, "What else did he put in, lamb?"

"Oh, lots and lots of things. One was a pretty blue can."

Martie Malone stood at the foot of the stairs. He took the sleep-flushed boy in his arms with a "How are they treating you, fellow?" Over the rumpled blond head he asked Beany, "Any word from Elizabeth yet about their coming for him?"

"In her last letter she said Don was much better and that he'd be dismissed from the hospital most any time. She said plans were still uncertain, but she hoped they'd be coming on real soon for a visit and take Martie home with them."

Elizabeth was the oldest of the Malone children. Johnny, who had a flair for words, described her as, "Loving, loveable, and lovely." So had Johnny tagged Mary Fred as, "Old bubble-and-bounce." And Beany as, "Our bossy little Beany—bless her!"

Elizabeth's wedding picture sat on the Malones' mantel. A young and radiant bride with a broad-shouldered man in a lieutenant's uniform. But Lieutenant Donald McCallin had received a shrapnel wound which necessitated the amputation of his leg below the knee. After his worrying convalescence, he, Elizabeth, and their small son had moved to Arizona.

Norbett, looking at the wedding picture one day, had said stanchly, "Elizabeth is even prettier than that now."

"I know," Beany had agreed. It was hard to put in words, but in the picture her young radiance seemed all on the outside. Now, after years of worry over a wounded soldier-husband, Elizabeth's radiance was the soft, yet strong kind, that came from the inside.

Elizabeth and little Martie had come home for a visit

in June. The plan had been that Don would drive up later and they would all go back to Arizona together. But Elizabeth had been at the Malones' only a week when she received word from Don that trouble had flared up in his leg again. He must go to the veterans' hospital near San Diego, where another operation might be necessary.

Elizabeth's one panicky idea had been to fly back. "Leave the boy with us until you see how things are with Don," Martie Malone had urged. "You'll be at the hospital most of the time and you'll be freer without the little tyke."

He meant, of course, You'll have enough worry about Don without worrying about who to leave the child with while you're at the hospital.

"Look," Johnny had added when Elizabeth hesitated, "he's as much our Martie as yours. We've raised him from a calf."

Beany's father said now, "We should be hearing from Elizabeth most any day."

Norbett got up as Beany, Martie Malone, and the little boy came into the room. "I brought you something, Big Ears," he said to the child, and drew out of his pocket a toy harmonica. "Sit up here and I'll show you how to blow it."

Small Martie turned it over in his hands. He said gravely, "This is nice, but the next time you come, will you bring some caps for my cap pistol?"

Norbett's eyes met Beany's. "No musician's soul," he grinned. "Just a gun-totin' hombre."

The boy sat between Beany and Norbett on the win

dow seat of the bay window, making experimental toots on the harmonica. Johnny was stirring sugar in his third glass of iced tea. Martie Malone started the leisurely ritual of filling his pipe, tamping it down carefully. He let the smallest member of the family strike the match and hold it to the pipe. The smell of pipe smoke filled the air like a heartening, assuring incense. He stretched out his long legs and a tired smile lighted his face. "Nice," he muttered, "to be in the thick of family again."

There had been a time when Norbett nursed an antagonism toward Martie Malone because he was top columnist on the *Morning Call* whereas Norbett was school reporter for the rival paper, the *Tribune*. A time, too, when Norbett had been jealous of Johnny and his happy ease in writing of historical events, which won him acclaim in high-school circles. All those things had made the course of true love run quite unsmooth for Beany Malone and the quick-tempered, hard-to-understand Norbett.

Yes, this was nice, Beany thought, but it'd be even nicer if Norbett would say, "How's about us taking a swim, Beany?" It was her vacation and Norbett's and she'd like to feel like a gadabout vacationer.

But Norbett swung the talk to newspapers and to the big anniversary number his *Tribune* would be getting out in September to celebrate its seventy-fifth year. He added moodily, "I've been beating my brains out, hoping I could come up with something—oh, maybe some new, old pictures, or a new, old story so as to get in that anniversary issue with a by-line."

"Hard to get anything new in the way of pictures." Johnny said. "Weren't too many photographers in pioneer days."

Norbett pursued, "Mr. Malone, you started in on the *Call* as a cub reporter, didn't you? Did it seem to you that you just kept right on marking time forever? I mean, I get discouraged because I'm still only an errand boy down there."

"Don't worry," Martie Malone said between relaxed puffs. "Keep your eyes and ears open and you'll break through with a big story that'll make them all sit up and notice you. Then they'll move you up a sizeable notch."

Norbett leaned forward tensely. "That's what I'm hoping. I stumbled onto something just this morning that might make a whale of a story—"

"But, Norbett, you're on vacation," Beany put in. "You said you'd have yours the first of July, and that's why I asked Eve Baxter if I could take mine then."

She blushed as she said it. Oh dear, supposing it was true that a girl shouldn't be so frank about such things. Kay Maffley's mother, who was forever telling about her innumerable suitors crowding her front porch when she was a girl, always gave Beany and Kay this maxim: "If you like a boy, pretend you don't. If you don't like him, pretend you do." But pretending came hard for any of the Malones, much less for a forthright Beany.

Norbett answered, "Yeh, my vacation started today but even so—"

"Even so," Martie Malone finished it, "a nose for news can't help smelling out a story, vacation or no."

Beany's father began a detailed story about his first break

on the *Call*. The afternoon wore on. Beany carried out the iced-tea glasses. Norbett got up to go. Beany's heart gave an uneasy thump. If only she had some future meeting to fasten to. She and Johnny followed him to the front door.

Beany burst out shamelessly, "Norbett, how about the band concert over at the park tonight? They're going to turn on the colored fountain—Johnny was reading in the paper about it."

Norbett didn't say, "That's a deal. I'll swing by and pick you up." He only stood there with that same absent look in his eyes.

Johnny filled in the breach. "I guess Beany and I'll drive over. Why don't you join us? We'll be in the back row—close to the popcorn stand—and guess why?"

"Okay, I'll drift over and hunt you up—unless," he added, "I should happen to get tied up on this hot story."

Beany said entreatingly, "Oh, let the hot story cool till morning."

As Norbett went down the steps, Beany thought, "I'll wet my hair and put it up on bobby pins so it'll look nice. I wish my white sunback dress were clean."

On that warm July night Beany sat on one of the many wooden benches with the hundreds of others under the stars and listened to the outdoor band concert in the park. She and Johnny, even as he had told Norbett, had chosen their place in the back row close to the popcorn stand. The inviting aroma of popping corn was in the air and Johnny's diligent crunching was in Beany's ears, even as the music flowed and swelled about them.

As folks milled by, looking questioningly at the empty

space beside Beany, she explained hurriedly, "We're sav-
ing it for someone." . . . Norbett had said he'd drift over
unless he got tied up on a hot story. . . .

Mary Fred had stayed home with little Martie because
their father had to go down to the *Morning Call.* "You two
go," Mary Fred had urged Beany and Johnny. "I've got
to wash and press clothes and sew on a few buttons. I might
even wrestle with a zipper if I feel ambitious though,
heaven knows, I'd have a better chance of wrangling one of
the wild broncs up on the ranch."

Behind the bandstand the colored fountain played.
Bright red sprays that looked like flame, orchid sprays that
looked like ostrich plumes, varicolored ones, that dipped
and swayed like dancers. Beany watched the fountain and
at the same time scanned every male figure that came
strolling along. She listened to the music but all the time
her ears listened for a familiar, "Hi, gal. Shove over a
little."

Sweet old Johnny, who didn't know "Yankee Doodle"
from Mendelssohn's "Spring Song," sitting there beside
her munching popcorn! She suspected that Johnny would
have preferred staying home and taking a rough trail with
his pioneers rather than the city streets that led to the park
and the band concert. Maybe Mary Fred had prodded him
into it with a, "Go on, you big lug, and take Beany to the
park. After all, it's her vacation." Maybe one reason Johnny
kept turning his head this way and that was a desire to turn
Beany over to Norbett so that Johnny Malone might hurry
on back to his maps and journals.

The girl soloist appeared and sang, "Ah, 'tis spring, 'tis
spring—Ah, ah, ah, ah—" Beany clapped with the rest,

but she would have felt more like spring, Ah, ah, ah, ah!—if
she were moving over to make room for Norbett.

And then the concert was over and Johnny was guiding
her through the leisurely throng to his little jalopy and
saying, "Let's stop at the Ragged Robin and have a coke.
Popcorn sure makes your gullet dry."

He wove his car through the tangle of park traffic and
up the broad thoroughfare which led to the Ragged Robin
drive-in. The Robin, as the high-school crowd termed it,
was a low, widespread building with an inside lunchroom,
with parking space outside, and an open counter at one
end where cokes, sandwiches, and desserts were dispensed.
Johnny managed to crowd into a parking space at the edge
of the lot. He said as he got out, "What'll you have,
mademoiselle?"

"Coke with cherry and ice."

With that a neon-lighted sign above the building flashed
on in front of their eyes. It showed a piece of pie with very
red, very juicy cherries, and a crust of tantalizing brown.
The piece of pie slanted into lettering which read, "Cherries picked this morning. Baked this afternoon."

Johnny said, "Cherry pie, huh! I do believe I could
manage a chunk. How about you, Beany?"

"No—just a coke."

But as she waited in the car, her eyes watched the sign
change from a luscious piece of pie to the luring words.
She felt her taste buds quicken in appreciation. She
climbed out of Johnny's car and started around to the front
of the building so that she could see Johnny and call to
him, "I'll have pie, too."

As she passed in front of the building, she glanced inside. Large, gleaming coffee urns with their trays of white, thick mugs and beside them, miniature bottles of cream. How intrigued little Martie always was with those toy-sized bottles! Next to the windows were small, intimate booths. Beany wondered idly why anyone would want to go inside and sit in the booths on such a warm night. But, of course, she knew the answer. It was cozier for couples who were "that way" about each other.

Beany's eyes rested on the couple sitting at the table inside the window nearest to her. For a half minute—though it seemed longer—her eyes registered the details of the picture framed by the window. The young man wore a pale yellow sport shirt. The girl opposite him was in a white sunback dress. Her hair was a smoky black and, now when other girls were wearing it short, hers was still long, as though such dark beauty could not be sacrificed to fashion's whim. Beany even thought, She doesn't seem to have as much trouble keeping that white dress clean as I do mine.

And then she found that her heart was beating hard and slow and that it was saying to her, "Why, that's Norbett Rhodes sitting there across from her!"

Involuntarily she stepped back into the dimmer light. As though Norbett would see her, she thought sickly. Norbett wasn't casting any glances around the room, or out of the window to see who was skirting across the front of the Ragged Robin. Norbett was leaning his elbows on the table and listening with rapt attention to every word the girl was saying.

Beany kept on backing away until she bumped into a car, her eyes still glued on that couple. She saw them get up

then. Or rather Norbett got up, reached for the check.
Beany saw the girl flash him a smile as she extracted her
compact from a white drawstring purse. While Norbett
paid the cashier, the girl bent over the mirror and carefully wielded a lipstick. Norbett waited indulgently for
this slow and painstaking job. If that was me, Beany
thought bitterly and ungrammatically, he'd be hurrying
me, saying, "Oh, come on—come on! The face you got is
good enough."

The two came out the door and the bright overhead
light revealed them like a spotlight. The objective part of
Beany's mind paid tribute to the girl's tumble of dark,
smoky hair, the dark eyes, the full lips made freshly red.
The light caught on her gold belt with a great hammered
buckle. She had gold sandals to match. Her tan was just
right. Not that dark sepia which was unbecoming, but a
smooth and satiny tan which made the white of the dress
whiter. She isn't the kind to freckle either, Beany thought
miserably.

They turned and walked on into the semigloom of the
parking lot. Oh no, that dress was not a white cotton sunback that one took off a rack with some thirty others. Its
very fit and hang and soft luster told Beany that its owner
had sat in one of the dress salons and had a clerk bring it
in to her and say, "Here is this original—it was featured
in *Mademoiselle* this month."

Beany was still pressed against the fender of some unknown car when she heard and recognized that special
lusty snort Norbett's car gave before it leaped into action.

She was still standing there when Johnny's footsteps
crunched through the gravel and Johnny scolded, "My

gosh, Beany, I been wandering all over the lot juggling this tray and looking for you. Here, grab your coke before it spills off. Why didn't you stay in the car?"

She didn't answer. Part of her wanted to lay her head on his chest and sob out, "I saw Norbett in a booth with a girl that's got everything I haven't. That's why he never came to the band concert." But some deeper hurt, some instinctive feminine pride kept her silent.

Johnny wended his way back to his own car and Beany followed. He dropped down on the running board, said, "I'm glad old Insomnia's got a running board. They're nice to sit on. Um-mm, this pie is almost as good as the ad looks. Want a bite?"

"No—no, I'm not hungry."

She sipped her coke. . . . "I'll drift over," Norbett had said, "unless I get tied up on this hot story. . . ." The coke had no flavor. A sliver of ice rasped as it went down her tight throat.

She had drunk only half of it when she said, "Let's go home, Johnny." She ached for the haven of her small room at the head of the stairs. She ached for its dark familiarity, for the feel of her own bed under her, for her pillow to burrow into—

Johnny took the remaining two square inches of pie and crust in one gulp, he drained his paper container of the last drop of coke, drained Beany's as well, and then tossed the paper cups over the car. "We're practically there, little Beaver."

3

BEANY PRAYS TO TAKE A TRIP

Beany came in the Malone side entrance while Johnny put the car in the garage. The steamy, hot smell of ironing met her as the screen door closed behind her. Mary Fred had the ironing board up in the small rectangular room between kitchen and dining room which they called the butler's pantry, in which, as Johnny always said, no butler had ever trod.

Mary Fred held up the red-plaid flannel shirt she wore with Levis and asked, "Look, little Beaver, does one iron this in the raw or should I cover it with a cloth?"

"You iron it on the wrong side," Beany said heavily. "And don't have your iron too hot. I guess I'll go to bed."

"I've worked up an appetite running a hand laundry. I'd eat a sandwich if you made one and thrust it upon me. Did Norbett come home with you?"

"No. He didn't show up at the band concert. Mary Fred,

there's cheese there—and rye bread. I'm going to bed."

She could feel Mary Fred standing beside the ironing board with the iron in her hand, looking after her as she walked through the back hall and toward the stairs.

In her dark room Beany dropped her clothes, felt out the armholes in her short-sleeved pajamas. Mary Fred came in softly, said in a whisper because little Martie's bed was crowded into Beany's room, "Beany, where are you?"

Mary Fred's arms reached out to the thin sound of, "I'm here on the bed—taking off my sandals. . . ." Not gold sandals—just green, scuffed ones. . . .

Mary Fred reached down and felt for the sandal buckles and, as though Beany were a two-year-old, she unfastened them, pulled them off. She felt for and turned back the sheet and yellow-plaid gingham spread and, still in that tone of maternal concern, said low, "Here, toots, climb in." She dropped down on the bed beside Beany's recumbent figure and said chidingly, "Beany, you aren't such a little sap that just because Norbett didn't show up at the park you think the world has come to an end? Is that it, petty doll?"

Beany couldn't answer for the hard lump, the size of a baseball, that formed in her throat.

Mary Fred patted her hand. "Tomorrow is another day. You get a good night's sleep. What d'you say we have pancakes for breakfast?"

Beany managed a thready, "That'd be swell."

Mary Fred sat on. She said then, "You know I'm so disappointed that we haven't got an answer to all those ads we've been running to locate Ander's roping horse. I know Ander's just heartsick."

Beany smiled wryly to herself. Mary Fred was trying to divert her mind. It was the same technique Beany, herself, used on little Martie when the galumphing Mike knocked him down, or when he pinched his fingers in the door. Beany always began talking fast about Peter Rabbit or Goldilocks breaking the little bear's chair.

"Did I ever tell you why Ander named him Quaker?" Mary Fred went on. "Well, it seems that when Quaker was just a colt his mother died—Quaker's—and so Ander raised him by hand. Sort of a *My Friend Flicka* deal, as I get it. And Ander used to feed him Quaker Oats that his mother bought for breakfast food. He said the colt liked them better than the regular grain they fed the horses—"

. . . The way Norbett had leaned across the table, his eyes so intent on the face of that dark girl. Just like a scene out of the movies. . . .

"—And the crazy colt got so he'd come galloping across the field the minute he saw Ander with a Quaker Oats box. Ander broke Quaker himself and he and some other prize roper taught him to be a roping horse. So much depends on the horse in roping. You know how the starter sits on his horse outside the chute they let the steers out of, and how he jerks the flag down the split second the steer crosses the mark. A good roping horse knows how to watch the flag and bolt off after the calf like a streak of lightning. And besides, a roping horse like Quaker knows when the loop settles over the steer's head and he braces himself and keeps the rope taut, so the steer can't start any funny business until the roper gets there to toss him down and start tying."

. . . Maybe they were still riding around in the red car. Maybe Norbett was saying, "There's your moon. Looks like a slice of honeydew melon, doesn't it? . . ."

"Poor old Ander is counting so heavy on winning some roping money. His folks have had a pretty rough deal on the ranch. They had a hail in June that just ruined their wheat. Ander says he hates to ask them to fork over money for this coming year. But he says there're about a half dozen rodeos with big prizes in different towns along the coast. If only we could locate Quaker! Ander thought he had a lead when he went up to his folks' ranch in Wyoming, but the card I got today said it was a false clue so—"

Beany burst out, "I wish I could take a trip. Everybody I know is going someplace."

"Oh gosh, lambie, I wish you were good around horses. If you were, you could go with me up to the dude ranch and get a job, wet-nursing the dudes that come out."

"But I'm not," Beany said flatly. "I'm even afraid of horses. They're so big and I always expect them to take a bite out of me."

"Oh, Beany, silly! They much prefer alfalfa. Well, look, Johnny's talking of going up to this Fort Bridger place in Wyoming, close to the Utah line, to find some more data on Jim Bridger. Why don't you go with him? And maybe the two of you could run on up and see your pal, Kay? Johnny used to think Kay was something, as I remember. At least you worked powerful hard to get him to thinking about her."

"She's got someone named Warren with a blue convertible to take her places now. Absence makes the heart grow fonder for somebody else," Beany repeated again and laughed so harshly that her small roommate stirred in his crib.

They sat very quiet until there was no squeak of springs in the corner, and then Mary Fred asked casually, "You didn't see Norbett at all this evening, huh? Well, he said something about being tied up with a hot story, didn't he?"

Beany meant her reply to be even more casual. "It wasn't a hot story that took up his evening—it was a hot date. If I ever saw a sultry number—" But, without warning, that lump, that baseball-sized lump, lodged in her throat and the last words came out in a strangled gulp.

"Beany, then you saw him? With another girl?" Unswallowable sobs shook Beany, and Mary Fred leaned over and laid her smooth cheek against Beany's wet one and said concernedly, "Tell me about it, Beany—tell your old Mary Fred."

Beany choked out the whole story in Mary Fred's arms. The cherry pie sign, and her skirting around in front of the Robin—the way Norbett had leaned across the table, intent on every word of the girl opposite him. Beany's laugh was ragged. "Her white dress wasn't any bargain rack one. It was the kind you have to send to a cleaner. I'll bet she's never had an iron in her hand."

"I know," Mary Fred put in with vehement sympathy. "She probably never lifted anything heavier than a bottle of bath salts." A long silence while Beany blew her nose and tried to steady the racking sobs that shook her. Then Mary Fred said slowly, "But look, little Beaver, it may not be too bad. After all, according to law, a man is innocent until he's proved guilty. How do we know but what this sultry fem was someone related to him—a cousin maybe?"

"He doesn't have any cousins," Beany said.

"Maybe she was someone attached to someone that came to visit Norbett's folks at the Park Gate, and they shunted them off together."

"Norbett isn't the kind that lets anyone shunt him off with someone. No, he's just tired of me—he's just giving me the push-off."

"Now, Beany, now," Mary Fred soothed. "Norbett isn't tired of you. You're just right for Norbett. Why, the old swell head is a different man since he's known you. He's almost human. He used to have the lousiest disposition of any two-footed critter. . . . The gal wasn't anyone you'd ever seen before, huh?"

"No . . . Mary Fred, you know Kay's mother? Well, she used to be quite a belle in her day. Men lined up on the front porch, and they brought her so many boxes of candy that she got bilious eating chocolates, and they sent so many roses it made her father's asthma worse. And she always said to Kay and me, 'If you like a boy, pretend you don't—' "

"Yeh," Mary Fred said, " 'and if you don't like a fellow, pretend you do.' That's the coy approach. But to me it sounds like tilted fans and sachets and corset covers. And besides it never seemed quite—cricket. It makes a girl's going with boys in the same class as fishing for trout. Try to fool them and hook them without their knowing it. Fooey!"

She remembered Martie in the corner, and lowered her voice to an emphatic whisper. "Look at Elizabeth. She had men keeping the telephone wires hot, and sending her violets and writing poems about her eyes being the same shade. No one had as many beaus as sweet old Elizabeth. Then she met Don—and they were crazy about each other from the start. Do you think she gave him that old razzamatazz when he called up and asked her if he could come out? She did not. When he said, 'I love you,' I'll bet she all but beat him to it. . . . Nosir, Norbett wouldn't have stuck around here like flypaper, he wouldn't have shaken out of all those moods and tantrums he used to throw, if you'd been the arch, 'Wonderful, loveable you,' one minute, and 'Sorry, but I've got another date,' the next. You made him peppermint-stick ice cream because he loved it, and he used to just lap it up—your making it for him, I mean, as well as the ice cream."

But that's all over now, Beany thought. She moved her arm and the charm bracelet seemed to clink drearily, "It's all over now."

Beany gulped, "I'm going to take off his old charm bracelet—and—and throw it in the ashpit. I just hate it—"

"You'll do nothing of the kind," Mary Fred said positively. "Don't you dare. Not until you find out for sure he gave you the run-around tonight. Promise me you won't, Beany."

Beany promised thickly and half-heartedly.

Mary Fred said, "I'd better get out of here before I wake up Big Ears over there." She stood up, gave Beany a loving clout on her behind, and bent to kiss her at the same time. "Now say your prayers like a good girl—and go to sleep."

She slipped softly through the door.

But Beany didn't say her prayers. She didn't go to sleep. Little events of the day kept leaping out at her and causing her to wince in humiliation. Oh, why had she told

Norbett that she had asked for her vacation at the same time his began? . . . Maybe Mary Fred's technique was all right for her and Ander. They could scrap and tease because they had that firm foundation of trust in each other. Ander would never tell Mary Fred he was busy and then hurry off to meet another girl. . . . Oh, why had she, Beany, all but asked Norbett to take her to the band concert? If only she could live the day over and act casual and uncaring!

She wanted to hurt him.

And then, suddenly, her wanting to take a trip, to go far, far away crystallized into an aching, informal prayer. She wanted to leave without a word to Norbett. Let Norbett stop and find her gone. Let Norbett say to Johnny, "Where's Beany?" and have Johnny say, "Oh, didn't you know? Beany's off gallivantin'." And Norbett would say, "She is! Well, I'll be doggoned—she never told me about it." And Johnny would say—she'd *coach* Johnny to say, "Oh, she was flying around here, happy as a lark and not thinking about anything or anybody but the wonderful time she was going to have."

And then—oh, if only Norbett would feel lonely and lost. If only he'd miss those evenings of making ice cream, miss having a Beany to listen to all his talk about his work at the *Tribune,* miss spilling out his unhappiness because his aunt and uncle, with whom he lived, were cold and ambitious and had no affection for him. "They just took me in when my folks died," Norbett always said, "because they'd have been ashamed to have folks know they sent me to an orphans' home."

Beany ached to go away. But where could she go? Not to

the dude ranch with Mary Fred, who rode off with city dudes on circle trips through the mountains. Beany would be more of a tenderfoot than the most citified Bostonian. . . . Not with her father while he sat in on the prison investigation. . . . She couldn't go with Johnny to Fort Bridger and Utah because someone would have to stay with Elizabeth's Martie. Even in her grief her tenderness flowed over to the crib and the little boy who was lying humped up in it. Over and over he would tag after Beany to ask, "Is Mommie coming for me tomorrow?" And Beany would answer, "Maybe the day after tomorrow, sweetie."

She heard her father come in and climb the stairs. He paused outside her door and again part of her ached for him to come in so she could say, "Father, what do you *do* when something hurts so hard you can't bear it?" She hungered to feel his hands tugging at her braids, hungered to hear him say as he patted her, "There, there, blessed!"

But because her grief suddenly made her older, she sensed that this was *hers*—her private heartache. Father's warm heart would ache with hers, and he'd had enough of burden and worry in mothering them and fathering them, as well.

His father's footsteps halted at Johnny's door. She heard their voices. Johnny, the night owl! He was probably sitting cross-legged on the floor, reading through the mass of old journals and diaries he had obtained from the library. Imagine anyone having shiny-eyed enthusiasm about an old scout, long since dead and gone. Then Beany heard the faint click of her father's typewriter.

She lay on wide eyed. Fool, fool that she'd been—wearing her heart on her sleeve, or where a sleeve would be if her summer dresses had sleeves.

And then, even before she heard the door knocker, she heard Red leave Johnny's room and go swiftly down the stairs with a low warning bark that almost said, "Be on your guard, everyone in the house."

A few seconds later the door knocker sounded.

Beany reached for her chintz housecoat and pulled it on as she raced down the stairs. With Red stiffened protectingly beside her, she opened the door. A man with a flashlight said, "The Malones? Airmail registered special for you. This was the last one on my route and I wouldn't have delivered it this late except I saw a light on and figured somebody was up."

The post office employee looked tired and wilted. He yawned widely as he pulled out a letter he had fitted into his cap and handed it to Beany.

He thrust a paper and a stub of pencil at her and said, "Sign for it there on the last line."

Beany didn't know that this yawning man in a damply mussed blue shirt was really an angel who was handing her, not a letter almost covered with airmail, registered, and special delivery stamps, but an answer to the longing that had ached through her, "If I could only take a trip!"

4

LETTER FROM ELIZABETH

Even as Beany closed the door behind the deliverer of the letter, her father was coming down the stairs, asking, "Is that a special for me, Beany? The committee was expecting to get some new evidence this afternoon and I suppose—"

And, at the same time, Mary Fred, pulling her white towel-robe about her, was shouting as her bare feet thudded down the stairs, "Maybe it's word about Quaker. Oh, if it is—late as it is!—I'll telephone Ander in Wyoming and have him come right down."

Johnny, too, was there demanding, "Who's it for, Beany? Who's it from?"

Beany moved closer under the hall light. "It's for me. It's from Elizabeth."

They stood about her while she opened the letter. A blue, folded check dropped out and fell on the floor. Johnny retrieved it, held it.

Beany read the letter to her listening audience.

Beany dear, and all you blesseds:

I have good news for you. The doctors have used one of these new drugs on Don so that all infection in his leg has cleared up. They won't have to operate. He'll be dismissed from the hospital any day now. And we have the most wonderful plans. An old school friend of Don's, a Captain Medina, has a beautiful big fishing vessel, and he's asked Don, our Martie, and me to go on a cruise with him. Nothing would do Don more good. Captain Medina will be leaving port the twelfth of this month. I have so much to do, for, although Don is better, he still needs looking after. So, Beany dear, I thought maybe you could bring little Martie and come out to San Diego on the train.

I'm enclosing the money for your round trip. I remembered your writing that you'd have a vacation the first of July. Sorry to be in such a rush. Wire me when you start and let us know when to expect you. My love to you all. What would I have done this last month without your caring for our little boy! Oh, Beany, we can hardly wait to see you and Martie.

Beany's hands were shaking so that Johnny had to reach out to steady the page for her. "Hey, there's a postscript," he said. "Read it."

Beany read,

P.S. We'll find you a nice young man to show you around out here in sunny California. Bring your swimming togs and freckle cream. You'll love the ocean.

Mary Fred reached over and pulled out the collar of Beany's flowered, chintz housecoat, which was lumped under, and impulsively kissed Beany's freckled nose. "There's your trip, little Beaver—all wrapped up and handed to you." And to her father and Johnny—"Our Beany's just been hankerin' to get away from it all."

Martie Malone's keen and kindly eyes rested on Beany's swollen face and red eyes. He reached over and grabbed one of her short pigtails and pulled her to him. "Why, my little," he said fondly, even penitently, "you *have* been staying put while all the rest of us go off in all directions. You'd like to go out to California and take Martie with you, wouldn't you?"

"Yes," Beany said in a voice that squeaked with excitement. A visit with Elizabeth and Don. The ocean. *And* a nice young man to show her around. She'd send post cards to everyone, "Having a heavenly time." Maybe she'd send one to Norbett—no, maybe just the silence of contempt for him.

Johnny opened the folded check. "Ninety bucks," he breathed. He turned it over and over thoughtfully and then asked, "Beany, would you rather go on the train or drive out in a car?"

"Why, in a car," she answered. For, somehow, her dreams of going away were connected with that special excitement of loading bags in a car, of adjusting sunglasses, of studying road maps.

"I've got an idea," Johnny went on. "I've been planning on going up to Fort Bridger to see if I can run down more data on my old pal, Jim. It's right on the road to California. Why couldn't Beany and I *drive* out and take Big Ears with us? It wouldn't cost any more for the three of us to drive out than it would for Beany to take the little guy on the train. My old jalopy is in good shape. We could see more of the country that way."

The Malone father began groping about his pockets. He said, "Johnny, see if you can find my pipe and tobacco. Let's sit down in the kitchen. Suppose we have a cup of coffee and talk this over."

The coffee percolated in swift tempo on the stove. The Malones talked even faster.

Johnny had produced a map, which he spread on the kitchen table. "Why, sure—sure. From Denver to San Diego is twelve hundred and sixty-eight miles. Let's see, if I get Insomnia's spark plugs cleaned, she can do—"

"Now wait!" Martie Malone said. "You'll leave that little puddle-jumper of yours at home. If you go, take the Dodge. I won't be needing it."

Father's saying they could take the Dodge was like his giving not only his consent, but his blessing. Beany pulled the road map toward her. Here was Denver, marked plainly with a circled red star. Black roads, red roads led off from it. Beckoning roads. . . . This same map in the days to follow was to be folded and unfolded, to become smudged with peanut butter, candy bars, spotted with soft drinks; was to wear through at the folds and be patched together with tape; was to carry pencil marks and close figurings on the margins and the pale blue expanse that was Mexico and the Pacific ocean. . . .

Everyone talked like characters in a fast-moving play.

Johnny: "Twelve hundred and sixty-eight miles. And our Dodge gets about seventeen miles to the gallon." (Business of figuring on the back of Elizabeth's letter.) "Eighty gallons of gas each way. Eighty times twenty-seven cents a gallon is twenty-one sixty. Say, twenty-five dollars for gas each way—"

Mary Fred: "Just today our dentist was telling me how he can make it out to California in two days. He gets up and leaves early one morning and he pulls in to Salt Lake in time for a late dinner. He takes off from Salt Lake in the morning and the next evening he's rolling into Los Angeles. San Diego isn't much farther than L.A."

Martie Malone: "Well, you two—three, counting Martie—needn't try to break any records."

Beany: "I could wear my green striped seersucker to ride in because it doesn't wrinkle. Or should I wear Levis, Mary Fred?"

Mary Fred: "The seersucker. Levis are hot. But stick in a pair just in case."

Martie Malone: "They have nice cottage-courts and motels all along the way where you can get a good night's rest."

Mary Fred: "I'll tell you what, Beany, you take that navy linen of mine and the chalky-white jewelry. I won't need it up on the dude ranch. Golly, if they weren't counting on me to come back and coddle the dudes, I'd love to go along with you."

Johnny: "We could lay over a day or two in Fort Bridger —no, I'll bet a day would be plenty for me to run down any material there. We'll ask Carlton Buell next door to water the lawn and feed the dogs while we're gone."

Beany: "I wonder if my old yellow swimming suit will do. It's kind of faded and grayish—"

Mary Fred: "It will not, puddin' head. You got it on sale and yellow was never your color. Elizabeth will trot out a nice young man for you. When you get out there you get you a glamorous and Hollywoodish swim outfit—something with green in it. You've got some money saved, haven't you?"

Beany: "I've got thirty-eight dollars that I was going to get glider cushions and a striped umbrella—but to heck with that. And I could do up my white dress and take it on a clothes hanger. You see tourists driving along with suits and things on hangers, so they'll be fresh when they get to wherever they're going."

Johnny: "And I'd say about eight quarts of oil would do it."

Mary Fred: "Yeh, take your white dress and I'll lend you my silver sandals and my silver and turquoise belt. You have yourself a real flingding when you get there."

Martie Malone: "Don't forget meals when you're hungry and motor courts when you get fagged driving. You'll want to deliver little Martie to Elizabeth and Don in good shape."

The clock ticked on, the coffee pot was emptied, the talk even ran down to fitful murmurs. And all the time the small person, around whom this whole trip was planned, slept blissfully on upstairs in Beany's room.

Finally Father tapped his pipe empty, gave it a few extra thumps on the heel of his shoe, and said thoughtfully, "There are two wonderful parts to any trip. One, planning for it and packing for it—and setting off. And second, and that's even better, the coming home."

Oh no, Beany thought, coming home will be an anticlimax. It's the going—and the seeing new places, new faces. And forgetting. Absence makes the heart grow fonder for somebody else. Look at Kay. It didn't take her long to start writing about a boy named Warren.

"And, of course," Martie Malone went on, "any trip is wasted unless you come home a little different and a little bigger person from the one you were when you started."

I'll be different, Beany thought. I'll have forgotten all about Norbett. When I see a red car in the street, I won't even look up. If this young man that Elizabeth finds for me is nice, I'll take off Norbett's charm bracelet and throw it in the Pacific Ocean.

"I wish we could start tomorrow morning," Beany said with a shiver of impatience.

Their father shook his head. "No, you'll need a day to get ready. Now scamper to bed, all of you."

They didn't scamper, but went on reluctant feet, hating to leave the road map, the delight of planning.

And even after Beany was in bed, she remembered something and got up. She crept through the house and out the back door. Roughly she thrust the newly painted chairs in a huddle and threw the tarp over them. One chair toppled over—but she didn't right it. The tarp wouldn't reach over the glider. But what difference did it make?

Good-by to ever finishing them. She was following the beckoning road. Good-by to that sappy little Beany who painted them with such joy because she planned outdoor suppers that would please one red-headed Norbett Rhodes. Good-by, and good riddance!

5

OH, QUAKER—MY QUAKER!

The next morning the Malones picked up the excitement of their plans for the California trip where they had
left off the night before.

They could scarcely settle to the breakfast pancakes
which Johnny baked with absent-minded exuberance.
"We're going to California," little Martie repeated over
and over in answer to their "Eat your breakfast, Big Ears."
Mike, the watchful, got more than his share of leftover
pancakes that morning.

Martie Malone stood in the middle of the kitchen, sip-
ping coffee and watching for the car which would take him
back to his job at the penitentiary. He said regretfully,
"I'm sorry I won't be here to see you off tomorrow. Now
Beany, you and Johnny spell each other driving. Don't
keep going when you're tired or hungry. Don't piece on
candy bars, or these ice cream sticks, but eat hot, filling
meals. Your reason for going is to deliver little Martie

McCallin to Elizabeth and Don in good shape. Keep that in mind."

"We will," Beany promised. "We'll take cushions so he can sleep on the back seat. We'll take a thermos jug of water."

Martie Malone took another sip of coffee, said, "Johnny, you take the Dodge up to Mac's garage and have him check it over. Here's enough money for an oil change, a lube job, a spare tire, and a battery charge. I want you to start out shipshape."

"Well-found, the old pioneers called it," Johnny grinned. "I was just thinking about Great-Grandfather Malone, writing in his diary, 'This trail West is a lot like the Trail of Life. So many are poor; so many are ignorant; so many are foolish. It's up to us who travel well-found to lend a hand to those who don't.' "

"The Malone hand lends easy," Mary Fred commented. "Great-Grandfather Malone landed here broke and hungry."

The car for which Martie Malone waited honked in the driveway. He said his farewells to them all and reluctantly left. He called back to Beany and Johnny, "Happy journey! Happy landing!"

Mary Fred hurried off to the dentist. Johnny took the car up to Mac's garage for the thorough checking over.

So many details of getting ready for a trip. And they all fell upon Beany, the practical. She brought down from the attic three pieces of luggage. This scuffed brown leather one Beany would pack her clothes in; the fiber one for Johnny, though Johnny had said, "Just throw in a couple of T shirts for me"; the small bag for Martie.

The washing machine chugged and swished. Beany's white piqué went into the first pristine suds. She couldn't help thinking, as it was sucked under the soapy foam, of that other white dress on the dark-haired girl—a dress so arrogantly right as to fit and soft fullness. She couldn't help the cold ache as she thought, "It's all over between Norbett and me."

Mary Fred returned from the dentist's at noon just when Beany hung her washing on the line. Young Martie "helped" by handing her the wringer-flattened clothes from the basket. They hung in graduated formation, Johnny's long-legged Levis, Beany's medium-sized ones, Martie's diminutive ones. The biggest T shirts, Johnny's; the medium-sized ones, Beany's; the smaller, almost handkerchief-sized ones, for the smallest passenger. The same with the socks.

The white dress she put on a hanger, saying admonishingly, "Now, Martie, we musn't let Mike out till the dress is dry."

Mary Fred stuck her head out the back door. "Our special blue-plate luncheon is now being served, Miss Malone."

But even when the tea was poured, the sandwiches made and cut into triangles, they were too fidgety to sit down and eat. They chided the small Martie, "Sit still and eat your lunch." Yet Beany would bob up to stand on the kitchen stool for lifting a thermos jug off the high cupboard shelf and ask, "The lid doesn't fit tight. Do you suppose it'll be all right?"

"Not for a long trip. It won't keep hot things hot or cold

things cold. Better get a new one. They had some on special at Downey's Drug."

Mary Fred would automatically leave the table to look out the window. "What do you suppose is keeping Johnny? I hope they won't find anything radically, meaning expensively, wrong with the car."

Beany, a sandwich in her hand, was shuffling through cans and packaged goods in the cupboard. "That's funny. Kay's mother told me she used to use almond meal and make a paste of it and put it on her face to bleach freckles. So I got some, and I was thinking I might take it along—"

"Sure, take it. Look as unspeckled as possible for your California man."

"It's disappeared. It was in a blue can. You haven't seen it, have you, Mary Fred?"

Mary Fred didn't answer. She was staring out the kitchen window, her eyes wide and staring, her mouth agape. "Beany," she gasped, "look here, and see if you see what I see." With the hand which wasn't holding her cup of tea, she brushed back a wisp of hair from her forehead, a habit she had when she was puzzled or amazed.

She muttered on, "It's almost like a mirage that I'm afraid will disappear. I've been hoping to see it for so long. A blue roan horse. He's in a trailer."

It was no mirage at which Beany stared. In the Malone driveway a dusty truck had stopped. Attached to the truck was a horse trailer and in the trailer was a stocky roan horse. A short man in farmer clothes, with a glum and set face, descended from the truck and stood studying the Malone residence, his eyes considering the front door, then the side door, then the back, as though he wasn't used to a house having three doors to choose from.

Mary Fred put down her cup of tea with a splash, and went out the back door, demanding excitedly as she went down the steps, "Is that Quaker? Has he got the Lazy E brand on his left hip?"

Beany followed. But she had to take time to put Mike back in; he had escaped when Mary Fred opened the door. He wouldn't answer to her call but romped about delightedly until Beany collared him and carried him, all wriggle and protest, into the house to be shut in the butler's pantry.

By the time Beany reached the scene of action the man had removed the endgate of the horse trailer, fastened it onto the back to make a slanting runway down which Mary Fred was backing the bulky horse. She turned a flushed and rapt face to Beany. "Isn't he a beauty? Look at those shoulders. Look at his muscles. Oh, and the wise, understanding look in his eyes!"

Beauty, Beany thought, is in the eyes of the beholder. Certainly the roan horse was broad of shoulder and muscles rippled under his roan hide. His eyes showed perhaps wisdom and understanding but also a mind of his own. But then all horses, it seemed to Beany on the few occasions when she had gone riding with Mary Fred, decided where they wanted to go and how fast or how slow they would proceed.

Once the horse was on the ground, Mary Fred ran appraising and loving hands over his back, his legs. Her fingers riffled the hair over the brand on his hip. "Yes, that's the Lazy E all right, and he's got two white feet and the mark in his forehead that Ander said was like a blurry seven." She beamed at the farmer. "Oh, I'm so happy that you brought him in today. Another day, and it would have been too late because I'm leaving tomorrow. I'll telephone Ander in Wyoming and he'll just burn up the road getting down. I can't tell you how much this roan horse means to us."

Beany squirmed uneasily. It seemed to her that in a horse deal it was poor business to let the horse's owner know how enthusiastic the other party was. Couldn't Mary Fred find a few defects to pick out? The bringer of the glad tidings, or rather the roan horse, didn't change expression. His set face with its downward creases only set, if possible, into firmer lines. Beany asked it, "How much do you want—I mean, how much are you going to charge for the horse?"

"D'you want the trailer, too?"

"Oh yes," Mary Fred said. "I'm sure we will. So Ander can take him back to Wyoming with him, and then on to California. Oh golly, I'd give ten dollars just to see Ander's face when he lays eyes on this horse!"

Beany crept close to Mary Fred to nudge her and mutter *sotto voce,* "Don't act so enthusiastic."

If Mary Fred heard she didn't heed, for she went happily on, "He's in wonderful shape—without being too fat. Ander was afraid he might be run down and would take building up before he could use him for roping."

The man offered laconically, "He's been running in my alfalfa field and coming up nights for grain."

Johnny came walking in the front gate. Mary Fred gave a hurried and delighted explanation to him, "It's Quaker!

Isn't that miraculous? Lazy E on the hip, blurred seven in his forehead. Oh, that reminds me! Ander said there was one acid test to follow to be dead sure. Beany, have we got a box of Quaker Oats in the house?"

Beany was guarding little Martie, who wanted to imitate Mary Fred in chummily petting the horse. "Can I feed him?" he kept asking. "Yes, we've got a box of Quaker Oats," she murmured.

"Quaker Oats box coming right up," Johnny said, as his long legs streaked toward the back door, as he took the three steps in one.

The farmer watched with only a faint lift of his boredom. Johnny emerged, carrying the familiar round box of breakfast food, with its trademark of red and blue background for the Quaker with his white bobbed hair and black hat.

Mary Fred took the box from Johnny. She held it out to Quaker. The moment was tense. Ander's next year of pre-med depended on whether or not the roan horse showed recognition of that box of breakfast food. Mary Fred shook the box. "Look, Quaker, do you know what this is?"

The horse looked at it, dropped his head to nibble gently and scratchingly at his foreleg. He switched his gray tail. His attention veered to the street where a huge, yellow truck lumbered by.

"Look at the box," prompted the little boy. "Lookit, Quaker!"

"We called him Jim," the farmer proffered.

"Maybe if you'd open it and let him sniff it," Johnny suggested.

"No, oh no," Mary Fred said troubledly. "Ander said he always followed him when he saw him with a Quaker Oats box. Of course, it's been a long time since he's seen one. They say elephants never forget, but I don't know about a horse." She rattled the contents of the pasteboard box again.

The horse reached a questioning nose out to it. Mary Fred took a couple of steps away from him. The horse seemed to consider a minute, his eyes on the bright box. Then, as the watchers held their breath, he took a step in her direction. Mary Fred walked on, backwards, the box under her arm. The horse followed, quickening his step until he could reach out and nudge at the box.

Mary Fred chortled with delight. "D'you see that? He's trying to nudge the box out of my arms. That's what Ander said he always did with him."

She opened it then, dipped her hand in and brought it out full. Quaker—for there was now no doubt about his identity—neatly dispatched the oats, wriggling his lips over her hand for every grain. "Oh, Quaker," Mary Fred breathed, "you beautiful, wonderful answer to prayer. The long quest is ended."

"You going to pay me for him?" the horse's owner wanted to know. "I got to get back to my farm by sundown."

Mary Fred stammered, "Well—you see, it's this friend of ours who wants the horse. He lives on a Wyoming ranch but during school he lives next door to us with his aunt while he takes pre-med. He raised Quaker from just a little colt and then he broke him into being a roping horse and, when he went in the army, he sold the horse. But if he has Quaker to ride he can win all sorts of roping money out in California."

"Where is this fellow now—whatever his name is?"

"Ander is his name—Ander Erhart. He's in Wyoming. He was down here and then he heard of a horse in Wyoming that sounded like it might be Quaker—but it wasn't. So he went back to his folks' ranch. It's not far from Laramie."

"I ain't got time to wait till he comes down from Wyoming. I'm milking nine cows. But when I saw your ad in the paper, I figured I could take time to load Jim up and bring him in."

Mary Fred said gratefully, "I'm glad you did."

Beany asked again, "How much do you want for the horse?"

"Ninety dollars. I traded a seventy-five-dollar cow for him last fall because I needed a horse to bring the cows in. I've fed him good all winter—and horses have gone up. You're getting a good buy for ninety dollars."

"I know," Mary Fred said faintly. "It's just that I— well, I thought Ander would be here to pay for him."

Johnny, who was the most impractical of all the Malones when it came to dollar signs, said heartily, "Yeh, ninety bucks for a good roping horse like Quaker is a good buy."

Beany groaned inwardly. Hadn't there ever been a bartering, horse-trading ancestor in the Malone family? Had every past and present Malone thought that the highest price was not too much to pay for what you wanted?

Beany said, "Mary Fred, why don't you go telephone

Ander right away and ask him what he wants to pay for the horse? Maybe he won't want to buy the horse if he has to pay *ninety* dollars for it."

But the owner, instead of weakening, said imperturbably, "If you want the trailer—well, I'll tell you about that trailer. I made it myself. Bought the wheels and tires and built it out of the best lumber I could buy. It ain't fancy, but when you buy one of these fancy ones with a hood to keep the wind off a horse, and all painted up red or yellow, you pay five, six hundred bucks for it."

"Oh golly," Mary Fred said thinly.

"But I'll let you have it for just what I put into it. And I ain't very keen about selling it either."

"How much did you put in it?" Beany asked. She reached out and grabbed little Martie back from the horse.

"Hundred and eighteen dollars."

"Mary Fred," Beany said desperately, "go right in the house and call up Ander."

"You wait here," Mary Fred said to the farmer, as though she feared he might load up the horse and disappear if she turned her back.

"I'll wait," he promised grimly.

The man hunkered down on the lawn that sloped toward the cement driveway. Beany, still keeping a watchful eye on Martie's friendly overtures to the horse, began picking off the line the clothes that were dry enough to iron. She took down the white dress. It was still wet around the hem but she had better not tempt fate further by keeping Mike and it separated. Yes, the silver belt and sandals of Mary Fred's would dress it up. . . . Gold belt, gold sandals . . . Again her heart gave a painful twist.

But anyway she hadn't thought about Norbett and his "hot story" for a long time. Not for all of the twenty minutes since the squat and stoic farmer had driven in with Quaker.

Mary Fred emerged from the side door, looking troubled. "I can't get hold of Ander. They have a phone on the ranch, but the operator can't get the call through."

"Wires probably down," grunted the man. He got to his feet and, farmerlike, cast his eyes to the sky. "The day's getting on. I like to get my milking and separating done by daylight. And one of my neighbors is coming over this evening to look at this roan. He figures on trading me hay for the horse and trailer for his son-in-law down near the Kansas line. Son-in-law needs a good horse for his two kids to ride to school."

Mary Fred said strickenly, "But this is Ander's special roping horse. And he's been looking and looking for him."

Johnny turned to the farmer. "Say, I bet you'd like a cup of coffee, wouldn't you? Come on in, and I'll have one for you in a jiffy—and a sandwich to keep it company."

Thus the horse-trading moved into the kitchen. Beany set up the ironing board and pulled her white dress on it, wrong side out. Mary Fred went back to the telephone in the hall. They could hear her prodding the operator, waiting, arguing with her all the while the coffee percolated. "You say a storm took the wires down? But we haven't had any storm down here."

"Had one farther north," the farmer said, stirring three spoonfuls of sugar into the coffee Johnny poured him.

"High wind and hail. No use trying to get them till some-body goes out and fixes the line."

Beany ironed on, her iron leaving a steamy path. Well, let the farmer take the horse back with him. Let Ander come down and deal with him direct. Maybe the neighbor wouldn't buy it *right away* for his son-in-law near the Kansas line.

Mary Fred, standing despairingly by the telephone, brightened. "I just happened to think. Ander's aunt, next door. I'm sure she'd be willing to pay for the horse and trailer. She pays that much for a little between-seasons suit without batting an eye."

"She left yesterday for a trip to Yellowstone," Beany imparted.

"Oh!" Mary Fred said flatly.

Then Johnny spoke up, Johnny, who hadn't a dicker-ing bone in his body. "Here's what I've been thinking," he said to the farmer. "Supposing we all pool all the dough we've got and give it to you, will you leave the horse and trailer here? We won't beat you out of a cent. I'll even let you take my jalopy as security for the rest. I've got twenty-two bucks. How much you got, Beany?"

"Thirty-eight dollars," Beany said reluctantly. The thirty-eight dollars the stay-at-home Beany had planned to invest in new cushions for the glider and a beautiful, striped, lawn umbrella. Thirty-eight dollars which the vacationing Beany intended using—or part of it—for a Hollywoodish beach outfit.

Mary Fred said hopefully, "I just got paid at the dude ranch before I came down. Let's see—I'd have more, only I paid my dentist—I've got forty-eight dollars and seventy cents. I can chip it all in because I've got my return bus ticket."

Johnny started adding aloud, "My twenty-two and Beany's thirty-eight is—is—"

"It all adds up to a hundred and eight dollars and seventy cents," Beany said shortly.

The owner of the horse and trailer took a sizeable bite of the sandwich Johnny had made, putting an inch-thick slice of meat loaf in it. He chewed on it while the three waited, while Beany thought grudgingly, "There goes my glamorous beach outfit."

Mary Fred, as though reading her mind, muttered, "You'll get your money back, Beany. You'll get it back right away from Ander." And in a lower and more earnest whisper, she added, "We can't let him take the horse and trailer away and sell it to somebody's son-in-law, can we?"

"Tell you what I'll do," the farmer said, his Adam's apple moving about in his throat and finally settling down. "I'll take your hundred and eight dollars. That'll be for the trailer. I guess I can knock off the other ten. I don't want to bother taking your car. Looks to me like you kids are honest—though I don't know about this cowboy you're talking about. I've seen cowboys I wouldn't trust any farther'n I can spit—"

"Then you'll leave Quaker with us," Mary Fred said eagerly. "Oh, wonderful!"

"Yeh, I'll leave him. But I got to have the ninety dollars for him in just a day or two."

"You'll get it," Mary Fred assured him. "Just as soon as I can get hold of Ander—they'll surely have the phone in working order by tonight! And I left the call with the operator—"

"He lives in Wyoming, huh?"

"Yes, not very far out of Laramie. It's only a hundred and thirteen miles from Denver."

"You give us your address," Johnny said earnestly, "and we'll have Ander come out and settle with you."

Johnny got pencil and paper and the man wrote down his name, "Oliver Hart." He added his box number on the R.F.D. route. He even wrote so as to make his house easier to find, "First white house after you pass the main-line ditch before you get to Gaffney."

He stood up then and said grimly, "This is Thursday and I'll give you till Monday. I'll come to town Monday morning and I'll stop here. Either I get my ninety dollars or I take the horse. But you can't go taking that horse anyplace. He's got to stay right here till he's paid for."

Mary Fred and Johnny walked out with him. Beany, watching through the window, saw them help detach the trailer. At last his dusty and crumpled truck rattled out of the Malone driveway. Mary Fred stopped to give Quaker a few loving pats before she came into the house with Johnny.

She asked, "Beany, do you know of a feed store any-where around here? We'll have to grain him tonight even though he can graze the lawn."

"We'll shut the gates," Johnny said, chomping a sand-wich, "and let him graze the whole lawn and then I won't have to cut it before we take off for California."

"They sell chicken feed up at the store on the boulevard where they sell ice," Beany proffered. "Would chicken feed do?"

"Johnny, will you drive me up to the chicken-feed, ice store?" Mary Fred asked.

"We'll have to walk up to the garage. I left the car there for Mac to check over." He finished off the half glass of milk in one long swallow. "Come along, then."

Mary Fred admonished from the doorway, "Don't get out of hearing distance of the phone, Beany. And keep an eye on Quaker."

6

A PAYING PASSENGER

Beany glanced out the window now and then to where Quaker nibbled at the grass. It wasn't a case of keeping an eye on Quaker so much as keeping an eye on young Martie McCallin. Once as Beany upended her iron and looked out she saw him holding out a ginger snap to the horse. The horse rumpled his lips over the ginger snap, showing great white teeth which looked to Beany quite capable of taking the small hand as well.

She hurried out and gathered the boy up—all protesting wail and flailing arms and legs—and brought him in. She put in a bad half hour getting him to settle down for his nap. His last reproachful words were, "Mary Fred said I could sit on his back."

"Well, take your nap, cutie, and when Mary Fred comes back maybe you can."

Beany returned to her ironing. She was putting the

white dress on a hanger when she glanced out again at Quaker. He was at the grape arbor, tearing off leaves and sampling the tiny beads of green grapes. Surely green grapes weren't on the diet of a roping horse. And besides, it was those grapes which would go into jelly for the Malones this fall.

She went out toward him. But he looked so—so unapproachable. She stood her distance and said, "Shoo! Shoo out of there!" Quaker turned his head and surveyed her boredly, a tendril of grapevine dangling from a corner of his mouth. Oh dear! Now if Mary Fred were here she would simply walk up and grab the rope tied to his halter and yank him to the spot where she wanted him. But could Beany? She wished Ander would hurry down from Wyoming and get his precious roping horse.

She heard the telephone pealing in the house and ran back to answer it. If this was Ander calling—and if Ander started right away he could be here by eight or nine o'clock, even if he didn't burn up the road.

She picked up the telephone. It was not Ander's voice but a woman's high-pitched one. "Is this the party that's driving to California?"

"Why, yes," Beany answered, mystified. "We're driving to California."

"What kind of a car are you driving?"

"A '41 Dodge."

"A '41 Dodge! Oh, I wouldn't want to go in such an *old* car. That's what my husband says, 'Don't go with anyone driving an old car, because you never know what will happen. So many things can go wrong with them.' But thank you just the same."

Even more mystified, Beany replaced the telephone in its black cradle. Must have been a wrong number, she decided.

She looked out the window again. Quaker, having sampled the grapevines and tiny green grapes, had now moved over to the tarp-covered furniture. He was scratching his shoulder on the back of a chair which protruded from the cover. Well, let him! This new, traveling Beany didn't care whether or not he rubbed off the soft coat of apple green which she had lovingly brushed on yesterday.

This new Beany had much ironing, much packing to do. She felt a moment of pushed and driven panic. The afternoon was well along and there were clothes for Johnny, Martie, and herself to iron, mend, and pack. She must see to all that, not only for her small nephew but for her tall, impractical brother. She must see that Martie's blond curls are cut. She must take her own huaraches to the shoe shop to have the strap stitched on. Oh yes, and the new thermos jug from Downey's Drug.

The telephone rang again and again, Beany raced to answer it. This time it was a man's voice, but not Ander's nice, familiar one. It was a throat-clearing, executive one which said, "I am calling in regard to the—ah-h—the party or parties who are motoring to California. Just who comprises this party?"

"My brother and I."

"And—ah-h—would you be kind enough to tell me your ages, please?"

"Why—why, Johnny's eighteen and I'm sixteen."

"Really! But I assume there are—ah-h—other passengers."

"Yes—little Martie."

"And may I ask how old he is?"

"He's four—almost five."

"H'm—h'mm—" a prolonged spell of throat-clearing. "Am I right in assuming that only you young people are starting off on this trip? Isn't there an older, shall we say, more responsible, person accompanying you?"

"No. No—just us—"

"Well, in that case—" Beany found herself clearing her own throat in unison with his—"I'm afraid we wouldn't be interested. I have considered—ah-h—procuring passage for my father with a responsible party but, inasmuch as he is—h'm—shall we say not too rugged, and well advanced in years, I'm afraid I wouldn't have perfect confidence in a party of—ah-h-h—such immature— However, thank you just the same."

"You're welcome," Beany said automatically. Though she wasn't quite sure for what the man was thanking her, or for what she was saying, "You're welcome." She started to ask, "How did you know we were going?" but the throat-clearer had hung up.

Again she replaced the telephone dazedly. Who were these mysterious people who wanted to know all the particulars about their trip to California? How had they found out in the first place? Beany thought of her friend, Kay, an only child living an ordered, apartment-house existence, who often sighed, "Things are always happening at the Malones'."

Kay was right. And sometimes a little too fast for comfort.

Was it only this time yesterday when the Malones, plus

Norbett Rhodes, had been sitting in the living room drinking iced tea? Days shouldn't be measured by squares on the calendar. Because in these last twenty-four hours, from the noontime of July first to the afternoon of July second, Beany Malone had changed from a busy, soft-hearted Beany to an even busier but hard-hearted Beany who would never put faith in a man again—at least not in a young man with hair the color of Red's and a change-able heart.

Her wiser-and-sadder philosophizing was interrupted by a kicking and scuffling at the back door. Mary Fred and Johnny—and a fifty-pound gunny sack of grain—almost fell in the door Beany opened. A red-faced and perspiring Mary Fred panted out, "Cracked corn. It was a chicken-feed place. And Johnny and I had to lug it for seven of the longest, hottest blocks I ever saw."

"You lugged it? But, Johnny, didn't you get the car from Mac's garage?"

Johnny only shook his head, as he reached for a glass and turned on the cold water.

Above the swish of water, and the rattle of pans as Mary Fred hunted for one big enough to feed Quaker in, the telephone bell sounded thin. "Catch it quick, Beany. Maybe that's Ander," Mary Fred prompted. "But don't you tell him about Quaker. I want to be the one to break the news to him."

Nor was this Ander's voice but a girl's voice which answered Beany's hello. "I've decided to go to California with you. When are you going?"

"We're going tomorrow, but—"

"Who's going?"

"Johnny and I. Oh yes, and little Martie."

"Little Martie! How old is he?"

Beany couldn't say why she felt an irritated antagonism toward the person who belonged to this young but assured and catechising voice. She answered shortly, "He's four. Almost five."

"Oh, I don't like—I mean, do you have to take a little boy along with you? Whenever I've gone anyplace with youngsters they crawl all over you—and they get sticky and cross, and they always want to stop to get a drink or go to a rest room or something—"

"Why don't you drive out all by yourself, as long as you're so particular?" Beany put in.

"I would, if I had a car," came the prompt answer. "I intend to pay you for taking me. Only I want to get there as soon as I can. Couldn't you send the little boy out on the train? Conductors are supposed to look after them."

Of all the nerve! Some strange and uppity girl calling up and practically ordering them to take her with them, and to send Martie out on the train! Because she didn't like sticky little boys. Beany snapped back angrily, "It so happens that the reason we're driving to California is to take Martie out to his mother and father."

And Beany did something that was seldom, if ever, done in the good-natured Malone household. She banged down the telephone viciously.

"It's the doggondest thing," Beany said as she walked into the kitchen. "The phone keeps ringing and ringing—and people keep asking me about our going to California. And telling me why they don't want to go with us.

You'd think we were down on our knees begging for a passenger to take along with us."

"Well, little Beaver, we are," Johnny said. "Not down on both knees—just one. We got to dig us up a paying passenger."

Beany stared at him. "What do you mean, Johnny Malone? We've got that money Elizabeth sent. You said it would be enough. You divided the miles by seventeen, which is what we get on our Dodge, and then multiplied it by the price of gasoline—"

"Wait, my pet, and I'll tell all. That is, if Mary Fred will stop clacking all those kettles and buckets long enough."

Mary Fred pulled her head out of the low storage space under the sink drainboard and, still on her knees but hunched back on her heels, said, "This canning kettle ought to be about right. Beany, toss me that tea towel to wipe out the dust. What did you say about being on one knee, Johnny?"

Johnny despondently sank into the nearest chair, gave out a long sigh, like the heave of a horse. "I took the car to Mac's to have it checked over. Father gave me the money to pay for an oil change, a lube job, a spare tire, and a battery charge. So far, so good. But when Mac took out the battery to give it a quick charge, by golly, the old thing practically fell apart in his hands." He dropped his own grimy hands helplessly, "Nothing to do about it— but get a new one."

"How much, Johnny?" It seemed to Beany that she had been asking, "How much?" all day.

Johnny winced as he said it. "Twenty bucks." He added hastily, "But it would have been twenty-two fifty, only Mac said he'd let us have it for what it cost him."

"Twenty bucks," Mary Fred echoed in a stricken whisper. "Gol-*lee,* that does make a dent in the ninety-dollar check Elizabeth sent."

Beany said. "But I still don't understand about the paying passenger and everybody telephoning about it *all at once.*"

Johnny grinned ruefully. "They always say radio advertising gets quick results. Here I was in the garage feeling frustrated and desperate, when who should come in, in his usual hurry-burry, but a fellow I know who works at a radio station. Ralph Everett. He was the one that had me cut a platter that time when I broadcast about early-day color and drama. I told him about our plans for going to California and how the horizon was suddenly darkened by our having to pay for a new battery. And Ralph said there were always passengers glad of a chance to pay—say, twenty-five dollars—to share a ride with someone."

"And did he broadcast that we wanted a paying passenger?" Beany asked.

"Must have. He promised he'd squeeze it in his next newscast if he wasn't too crowded for time. He said he'd say, 'Like a trip to California? If so, contact the Malones, who have room for a paying passenger,' and he'd give our address and phone number. So don't be getting snippy, Beany, with any prospective customers. What'd this last one sound like?"

"Like the Duchess of Castlemaine. Like a spoiled brat,"

Beany said. "But, Johnny, supposing we don't get a pay-ing passenger, what'll we do?"

A sober silence fell on the three in the kitchen. There was only the soft swish of Mary Fred's tea towel as she wiped dust out of the big, enameled canner. Johnny said, "Father gave me what he thought would be plenty to get the car in shape. I can't ask Mac for credit because he has to buy the battery himself. I suppose we could send an SOS up to Pop at the pen but, after all—"

"Oh no, I don't think we ought to," Beany said slowly. The Malone children had been brought up to get them-selves out of life's jams. As Johnny once put it, "We don't have a mother's skirt to hang onto, and Pop not only moves about so fast but he has the world hanging onto his coat tails."

Johnny asked, "Three calls you said you got on going to California with us? What'd they say?"

"The first one didn't want to trust herself with such an *old* car. The second didn't want to trust his father with such *young* people. And this last one—well, I wouldn't trust myself around *her*. Imagine her saying she didn't like children. Telling me we should send him out on the train. Why else," she added indignantly, "are we going to California except to take little Martie? . . ." Well, for one other reason which Beany wasn't putting into words: so that Beany Malone could put miles between herself and her disillusioning past. . . .

"We'll get more calls," Johnny said optimistically. "Ralph Everett said the town was full of people who'd give a bicuspid—even throw in a wisdom tooth—for a chance to go."

But the evening wore on. Not once again did the telephone ring. No long-distance call from Ander Erhart in Wyoming. No passengers who would forfeit a bicuspid to go to California. Though the Malones would settle for twenty-five dollars.

They ate supper, listening, hoping to hear the telephone's peal. They washed dishes and wiped them as quietly as possible so they'd be sure to hear it.

Beany rocked little Martie. But he was too excited about the trip to succumb to sleep. Beany sang his favorite, "Red Wing."

*"Now the moon shines tonight on pretty Red Wing,
The breeze is sighing, the night birds crying—"*

Ordinarily that line had to be changed to, "The night birds are *not* crying," because he couldn't bear to think of birds crying. But this evening when Beany absent-mindedly sang it without injecting the "are not" the little boy didn't notice. For he was mumbling, "I can take my gun, can't I? When do you think Norbett will bring me the caps to shoot?"

Beany was just answering for the fourth time, "I don't know," when the door knocker sounded.

Beany opened the front door with Martie, in blue cotton sleepers, crowding close. It took Beany's eyes a full and surprised minute to take in everything she saw before her. A gray-haired, pink-cheeked, comfortably plump woman stood there smiling at Beany out of kindly, childlike blue eyes. She was breathing hard from walking and carrying—how had she ever carried all those cartons and shopping bags, every one of them bulging?

The woman disengaged from her wrist one lopsided, clinking mesh bag and leaned it against the doorway, before she smiled again at Beany and said simply, "I'm Miss Opal Macafee. I came out to go to California with you."

"You did! I mean—you are!" Beany gasped.

"That's right, lovey. I just happened to hear it on the radio, and I swear to goodness, it sounded like the voice of Fate, saying, 'There's the chance you've been looking for, woman. So hurry about and get ready.'"

But Beany, having suffered three rebuffs from tentative passengers, said, "Well—wait, Miss Opal. Maybe you won't want to go out with us. We're driving out in a '41 Dodge."

"Oh, that's nice. One of my boys always said there was never a finer car made than a Dodge."

"One of your boys? I thought you said *Miss* Opal?"

"That's right, dearie. I'm Miss Opal but I have two or three boys that I've looked after and schooled and I always call them my boys. But they're grown now and I'm alone, except when one or the other of them come back to visit me."

"Oh!" Beany said.

Beany added, "And Johnny and I are going to do the driving. Johnny's eighteen and I'm sixteen—and there isn't any mature or more responsible person going along with us."

"You look pretty responsible," the woman said comfortably, "and is this Johnny?" For Johnny had come into the hallway. "Johnny looks fine and trustworthy, too." She put out her hand and said to him, even as she had to

Beany, "I'm Miss Opal Macafee. I came to go out to California with you."

Johnny beamed back at her. "You did? That's swell. We've been wanting another passenger."

But Beany pursued, "And another thing, Miss Opal. Martie here is going with us. That's why we're going out —to take him to his mother. But I guess some people don't like to have little kids crawling all over them—and they *do* get sticky and cross when they're sleepy. And they're always thirsty or else wanting to stop to go to the rest room or—*something.*"

"Bless them," she said fondly and, stooping, pushed the little boy's blond hair back from his forehead. "You ought to be in bed, codger." She gave him a roguish wink. "Did you ever hear the song about hanging Samuel Hall?"

"I want to," he said earnestly. "Did they hang him dead?"

"Stone-cold dead," she assured him.

Johnny was explaining, "We didn't think of taking a —a paying passenger, until we had to pay out for a new battery. I suppose we could have got hold of Father with an SOS—but he's got enough on his mind with this penitentiary probe he's on. So we figured we could make it, neat as a pin, by taking a paying passenger."

Miss Opal asked soberly, "How much do you want your paying passenger to pay?"

Johnny hemmed and ran his hand through his dark thatch of hair. It was always difficult for Johnny, even as for all the Malones, to talk money. Especially to a kindly, trusting-eyed woman like Miss Opal. "Well—you see— the new battery set us back twenty bucks—"

Even Beany had difficulty in saying, "The radio news-caster said it was worth twenty-five dollars. He said a lot of people would give a bicuspid to get a ride out and back for that."

"It's well worth it," Miss Opal assured them. "Only I don't have a bicuspid. And I don't have any cash. But I thought I could make it up by bringing along some pro-visions. I live on a little farm, so I killed some of my plumpest friers. I brought five, all fried and ready to eat. I mixed up some bread and roll dough but I didn't take time to bake it. And some canned fruit and jelly. I fig-ured it'd save you from paying out for meals along the way."

Mary Fred came in from her last good-night to Quaker. Miss Opal turned to her and smiled. "I've never seen such pretty eyes as you children have. Long lashes. My mother used to say that folks who had long lashes were always shielded from seeing the ugly things in life. And I've found it so."

Johnny murmured, "It'll be nice to have fried chicken to eat along the way."

"And I brought something else that'll come in handy on the trip." Miss Opal stepped back to the porch and tugged into the light a large, wooden bucket out of which grew what seemed, at first glance, a huge bush. Closer inspection showed it to be a sturdy, though slightly wilted, tomato plant with round balls of green and pink tomatoes on it.

Miss Opal said proudly, "I'll bet there's not another tomato plant in the state that's bearing tomatoes on the second day of July. But I'll tell you what I did. I've got a

big south window and flowers grow in it just as though
it were a hothouse. So I started this tomato plant inside
before the snow was off the ground. As it grew out of one
pot, I'd change it to a bigger one. I transplanted it outside
during that warm spell in May. And then when I decided
to go to California with you folks, out came my shovel
again and into this big bucket it went. There's nothing
so thirst quenching and refreshing as a tomato right off
the vine, I thought to myself."

Beany said impulsively, "Oh, we'll be glad to have you
go with us."

"I'll get all this stuff into the hall," Miss Opal said.
"It looks a little like rain."

They all helped her. As Beany and Mary Fred tugged
at a carton, full of jars of fruit, Mary Fred giggled softly
and said, "Heaven help us, you'd think you were going
overland in a covered wagon with all this canned fruit,
bread dough—and that tomato tree. Why, as my dentist
says, you can make it in two day-long hops with just that
overnight stop in Salt Lake."

7

CALIFORNIA, HERE WE COME!

Miss Opal wore a flowered voile dress which she had very evidently stitched up on her own sewing machine, cutting it off the same pattern she had used for years. Gathered skirt, long full sleeves, lace vest and collar. No doubt, Beany thought defensively, a fashion expert would wince at a woman of Miss Opal's ample proportions selecting dress material in which oversize lavender tulips ran riot.

Her black hat had seen years of service. It was only the flowers, Beany realized, which blossomed anew on it every spring. This spring Miss Opal had chosen pink, yellow, and blue daisies.

But the item that attracted Beany's attention and wonder was the belt which encompassed Miss Opal's waist. It was a wide red-velvet belt with a large velvet-covered buckle.

Miss Opal came into the house with her hat on, with the sleeves of her dress buttoned at the wrists. But the next time Beany looked at her, the hat was off, the sleeves were rolled up, and she was moving deftly about the kitchen. She said, "First off, I'll make this bread dough into loaves and rolls, and while it's raising, I'll get this wide-eyed little chap to sleep."

Their biggest bread pan held four loaves of bread, two cookie pans were full of rolls, when she washed her hands and turned to the tagging Martie to say, "Come on now, and I'll sing you about hanging Samuel Hall and his hatin' one and all."

The rain she had predicted began to patter, then pound on the roof as she rocked the little boy, singing songs first which held his interest and then gradually shifting to soothing lullabies. Martie's eyes, in spite of his determination to stay up and get ready to go to California, couldn't stay open.

Quite amazingly Miss Opal could, without breaking the rhythm of her rocking or the melody, offer counsel to Beany and Mary Fred and Johnny. "Best take a blanket or two with us in the car—'The robins so red, brought strawberry leaves and—' You never know when you'll need one on a trip. '—and over them spread—' Mary Fred, if you'll find the blue button off your blouse, I'll sew it on. Johnny, sample a roll or two if you'd like."

She was folksy and motherly, as though she gave a nice cluck-cluck and said, "There now, my wings are broad enough to cover you all." And the Malone hearts felt warmed and heartened by her presence.

Little Martie slept, a limp weight in her arms. Her

voice stilled. Johnny asked, "Where are you going in California?"

"To Oceanside. That's between San Diego and Los Angeles. I'm going to a little fruit ranch a few miles out of town."

"Oceanside isn't a bit out of our way," Johnny assured her. "We'll go through there, going to San Diego."

"Are you going out to visit relatives?" Beany asked.

"No, pet, I don't have any relatives out there. My going is what you might say a sentimental journey. Or maybe you'd call it keeping a covenant. An old friend of mine died last winter, and he asked me to go out to where he had lived and divide up the few little things he left. Mostly letters and keepsakes, and a few gifts he wanted to give to folks who had been good to him during his lifetime."

Beany wanted to ask more about this sentimental journey but Johnny said, "I'll carry Martie up to bed. He's quite an armful."

The child stirred and Miss Opal's rocker creaked gently again in time to, "Those poor little babes—those poor little babes—" She said softly, "No, it's best if I carry him so as not to disturb him. Show me where to put him, Beany."

Beany led the way up the stairs to her small room. She turned back the light blanket while Miss Opal, panting from the exertion, eased the little boy into his cot in the corner. He never stirred as Beany covered him.

Miss Opal looked around Beany's softly lighted room. This small room had once been the nursery annex to the two-room suite which adjoined it. Beany, as the baby of the family, had been the last one to occupy it. The room had grown up with Beany. The baby crib had been replaced by a cot, the cot by her three-quarter bed.

The junior-high Beany, irritated by the nursery wallpaper with its border of rabbits, had decorated the room herself. Beany liked this little room because it was at the head of the stairs. In it Beany could keep her finger on the pulse of all that went on in the Malone home. On the sleeping porch of the two-room suite, Mary Fred could sleep through telephone calls or the clack of the door knocker. But here Beany could hear Johnny pounding on his typewriter, could hear her father's step on the stairs when he came in after working late at the paper.

Beany's door didn't even shut tight. It was always her door through which Red pushed, always Beany's bed that he put his big paws on, Beany's face that he nudged when something untoward happened, as though Red sensed that next to him, Beany was the most alert one in the house.

Miss Opal whispered, "Ah, this is a dear little room."

Beany murmured, "I fixed it up myself two or three years ago. I read an article in a magazine about how yellow plaid curtains and bedspread and dressing-table skirt would pull the sun right out of the sky and bring it into the room—"

"And happiness with it," Miss Opal said.

"Yeh—" Beany said dubiously. But there had been no happiness in the room last night, when she had turned and tossed in bed, alternately wincing and aching. Wincing at the thought of her throwing herself at Norbett, aching with hurt and jealousy of that dark-haired siren Norbett had spent the evening with.

They walked down the wide stairs. At the foot, Miss

Opal paused and looked into the big beamed living room with its seven-windowed bow taking up half of the south wall space. At the generous fireplace over whose coals hundreds of wienies and marshmallows had been toasted. At the couch and easy chairs with their slipcovers, faded by wear and washings.

"This room," Mary Fred had once said ruefully but fondly, "may not look like the rooms which have 'personalized decoration' but it has just the same." She meant, of course, that everything there was for reasons of comfort or sentiment. The scuffed red leather chair that their father always made for because the hollows had formed to fit his tall figure. The white bear-rug which some explorer friend had sent him. (Most of the bear's teeth were out and bare spots showed through the fur.) The picture of Mary Fred's beloved horse, Mr. Chips, and the trophies she had won in horse shows. And the candelabrum Johnny had made in metal craft at school and brought home to his mother.

Miss Opal turned to Beany to say, "It's a sweet home to come back to, child."

Come back to? Beany's only thought was of leaving.

Beany was wakened out of a sound sleep the next morning by Mary Fred's shaking her. Beany jerked up sleepily and with a start.

The mere fact that Mary Fred was up and about was, in itself, startling. For Mary Fred was the slugabed in the Malone family. She was the one who always said, "Now I'm going to get up early in the morning," and then had to be pried out at the latest possible moment.

Mary Fred was saying urgently, "Beany, you've just got to take him to Wyoming with you. There's no two ways about it. I stayed up till way past midnight, trying to reach Ander. And I was up this morning before the larks were on the wing, working on the telephone operators. But we can't get a call through."

Beany blinked fast, trying to focus her eyes on Mary Fred's tense face, trying to focus her mind on Mary Fred's words. "You mean take Quaker to Wyoming as we go? Oh gosh! I thought this was my vacation. I'd rather have an albatross around my neck than a horse."

"I know you don't vibrate to horses, Beany, but think of Ander's whole future. It's only a measly hundred and thirty-eight miles to their ranch. You just go through Laramie and—"

Beany interrupted, "But we can't take him. The farmer said we couldn't take the horse out of the state."

"I know he did," Mary Fred said helplessly. "But what else can we do? I have to take the bus at noon, and we can't just leave him here, can we? And besides, the farmer said he'd be back in four days. Well, Ander will have the money in his hands before then. He'll mail it right down. And besides—well, it's Ander's horse that he raised from a colt."

"But we can't take him," Beany interrupted hopefully again. "You have to have a regular gimmick on your car to fasten a trailer to. It has to be welded on."

"No, it doesn't. You can get a trailer hitch bolted onto the rear bumper. Johnny's getting it put on now. I routed him out early, and he's up at Mac's garage—" She stopped in obvious embarrassment at Beany's accusing glare, and hurried on, "Honest, chick, it was the only thing to do. It won't take long. He'll be through by the time you get those extras up on the boulevard."

Beany couldn't help throwing back the covers with a despairing flip and landing on her feet with an irritated thump. "Oh now, Beany," Mary Fred reasoned, "don't act like an early Christian martyr. If you knew how I wish I could go as far as the Erhart ranch with you! But I can't. They strained a point, as was, letting me come down to have my tooth filled. But, jiminy, I'd love to see Ander's face when you drive in with Quaker."

Beany conceded, "Well, I suppose we could take him with us for a hundred and thirty-eight miles."

Mary Fred followed up her vantage point. "I'll feed him and water him before you go. You won't even know he's there in the trailer behind your car. And Ander will pay you and Johnny what you paid for the trailer, and you'll have it for your swanky beach outfit. Hey, stick your head out the door and sniff the heavenly smells coming up from the kitchen. That's your Miss Opal at the kitchen stove, working miracles with waffles and sausage."

Young Martie was awake by now. Mary Fred bent over his crib and scooped him up. She reached for his diminutive Levis, blouse, and sandals. She said as she roughed up his golden halo of silken curls, "Better take him to the barber shop, Beany, when you go up to the boulevard for the thermos jug. You know how his father feels about a boy looking like a girl-angel on a Sunday-school card."

"I know," Beany sighed. It was always a wrench to see those blond ringlets snipped off. She rationalized, "It'll be easier to keep combed on the trip if it's short."

So many things to do—to get. The word had got out
that they were driving to California and more experienced
travelers kept advising them, "Be sure and take dark
glasses." "Be sure and wear comfortable sandals or huaraches." "Be sure and take fruit along for Martie."

Mary Fred spent the morning working over the horse
trailer. She climbed over it and under it, tightening bolts
with a wrench. She smoothed down rough spots that might
possibly rub or scratch the roan hide of Quaker. The top
boards, where his shoulders touched, she even padded with
torn strips of old sheets.

She called after Beany as she set out for the boulevard
with Martie, "Beany, get a couple of big cartons of Quaker
Oats for him. He doesn't like this cracked corn very well."
And when Beany passed Mac's garage where Johnny was
overseeing and helping the mechanics with the trailer
hitch, he came to the door to say, "Beany, get a five-pound
package of frozen horse-meat to leave with Carlton Buell
next door to feed the dogs while we're gone."

The morning grew hotter and sultrier as Beany sat in
the barbershop and watched wispy blond tendrils fall
about the barber chair in which Martie squirmed; as she
shopped at first this store and that for a gallon thermos
jug; as she waited at the shoemaker's for his stitching the
straps on her huaraches. The little boy's legs were tired
before she completed her stops at the grocery, pet shop,
and the small dry-goods store for new Levis for him.

What an awkward and staggering load she had accumu-
lated. The thermos jug was packed in a large, squarish
carton that bulged out one arm. The two round cartons of
Quaker Oats kept sliding around under the other arm,

which also had to hug the grocer's sack with "the fruit to take along," as well as the rocklike package of frozen meat, which chilled her through her thin T shirt. The huaraches, which she had looped over her wrist, slapped against her as she walked.

Martie tagged behind her. He had been enthusiastic at first about carrying the package containing his new clothes, but his enthusiasm diminished at the end of the first block. He said plaintively, "Aunt Beany, I'm tired. I don't want to carry this package. It's heavy."

"I know, sweetie, but I can't carry another thing. It's all I can do to manage what I've got. My arms are tired, too."

In fact, it was more than she could manage, as she realized after picking up a carton of Quaker Oats for the third time. She had to ease all her load out of her arms and onto the curb. Martie took that opportunity to sit on one of the round boxes of breakfast food.

Let's see. If she took the thermos jug out of that unwieldy carton, she could more easily carry it by the handle. And why couldn't she take the two pairs of dark glasses out of the boxes they came in and which bulged the pocket of her full skirt? She could wear the two pairs until she got home and, by so doing, could squeeze Martie's package into her pocket.

With the two pairs of glasses on, she bent over and ripped open the well-sealed carton. She was trying to extricate from its snug nest the round, insulated jug when her eyes, even behind two dark layers of lens, caught a flash of red car in the street. But then, of course, her heart registered its usual skip-stop beat at the same time.

It was Norbett Rhodes and he stopped the car with his usual abruptness—like yanking a horse up on its haunches.

Norbett Rhodes! The one person whom two days ago Beany would have been most happy to see. The one person whom she was most unhappy to see this morning. Because she hoped to be far along the road to California before Norbett even knew she was going. She hoped that Norbett would telephone the Malone residence again and again without getting an answer. And that he would drive to their house and find it closed with the draperies drawn. She hoped he'd query Carlton Buell, who would probably be feeding the dogs or watering the lawn, "Where is Beany?" And that Carlton would answer, "Oh, didn't you know? She went tripping off to California."

I won't say a word to him about going away—not a word, she was vowing as Norbett climbed out of the car and came toward her. "Hi there, Queenie!" he greeted her jovially.

"Oh—good morning," she said thinly.

"Hey, take off a couple pair of those blinders and maybe you'll recognize me. You've seen me before. Norbett Rhodes, graduate of Harkness High—remember? Looks like you could stand a lift."

"No—no, thanks. I've got a few more errands to do yet. It's just a step and I—I like to walk. These things look heavy—but they aren't, really. And I'm not a bit tired."

"Yes, you are, Aunt Beany—you said you were. You said your arms hurt," her small companion interrupted.

Norbett said peremptorily, "Come on and get in." He

picked up the thermos jug, the cartons of Quaker Oats, the knobby, lopsided sack of fruit, the frozen meat for the dogs. "You don't think I'd let my girl walk home, loaded down like a pack horse, do you?"

His girl! Two days ago those two words would have warmed the furthest corners of her heart. But not this morning. It was all she could do to refrain from flinging out, *"Your girl!* Your girl would never be loaded down like a pack horse. She wouldn't be carrying a pair of beat-up huaraches that the shoemaker had to sew together."

But she said nothing. Even when he said in his old way, "New thermos, huh? Going on a picnic?" she didn't answer. She wouldn't breathe California, and then when Carlton Buell told Norbett she was gone, he would be even more amazed. And, she hoped, hurt. He'd mutter, "Well, that's funny! I saw her with a new thermos and dark, driving glasses, but she never gave a peep about going anyplace. . . ."

But what Beany proposed, little Martie disposed. He announced in his booming voice as he climbed with alacrity into the red car, "Norbett, I need caps for my gun. We're going to California. Aunt Beany and me and Johnny."

"You are?" He turned an incredulous face to Beany. "No kidding, Beany? When are you going?"

"Oh—today." Very casually, as though going that twelve hundred and sixty-eight miles was an everyday occurrence.

"What are you going for?"

"To take Martie home," she said laconically. . . . To get away from you, she thought. . . . She added, "I just got fed up on staying home and seeing the same old people."

He looked at her set face around the two pairs of dark glasses, and a baffled and angry look came into his dark, hazel eyes. Beany felt him stiffen. Even then Beany hoped he might say, "But, gosh, Beany, I'm having my vacation, and I thought we could take a few jaunts together." If he had—well, Beany didn't know what thawing effect that might have on her. But instead he said coldly, "That's nice. I'm sort of halfway planning to dash out there myself."

He swished up the Malone driveway, stopped with such a jerk that both pairs of Beany's glasses dropped off. Before she could gather them up off the floor, the little boy spilled out more information: "And we're going to take Miss Opal." He ran the three syllables together in one word.

Norbett asked, "Who's Misopal?"

"Miss Opal," Beany enunciated clearly. "She's a passenger we're taking out to California with us."

"Miss Opal!" he exclaimed. "Is her last name Macafee?"

"Yes, it is."

"Holy Smoke! Miss Opal Macafee. You can't take *her*, Beany."

"Why can't we?"

"How did you ever get mixed up with that woman? You take my advice and drop *her* like a hot potato."

Beany felt her temper rising. She started to flare back, "She isn't the one that ought to be dropped like a hot potato." But she got only two words out when she checked herself. Mary Fred always said, "When bigger battles are fought, Beany and Norbett will fight them." Well, she wouldn't lower her dignity to fight with Norbett this morning. It would probably be their last—their very last—meeting and she'd be cool and uncaring, so that he would always remember *that* Beany.

Martie vouchsafed, "Miss Opal came to our house and said she was going with us."

"How'd she know you were going? But *she* would! She's like an old witch with a sixth sense that knows everything."

Beany said shortly, "She didn't have to have a sixth sense. Just a radio. We needed a paying passenger, and a friend of Johnny's broadcast it and so—"

"You don't have to take her. But that's just like you Malones to pick up any Tom—I mean Miss Tom, Dick or Harry. Why, you could get a dozen passengers, but no, you would have to pick her."

"It wasn't a question of our picking. One party wouldn't trust herself to go in our old Dodge, and another wouldn't trust his palsied father with young drivers. And one perfectly nasty girl wouldn't think of going if we took Martie, for fear he might touch her sacred person with a sticky hand and—"

Norbett interrupted, "But, Beany, you don't know a thing about this Miss Opal person."

"We certainly do. She lives on a little truck farm at the edge of town, and she helped to raise four—well, anyway some boys, and put them through school."

"And she brought a tomato tree in a bucket," Martie volunteered. "And it's got little tiny tomatoes—and we can just reach out and take bites off them."

Beany said hastily, "Here, Martie, you take this package

and go show Mary Fred your new overalls." How could
one carry on a lofty argument with his childish prattling
about a tomato tree from which they could eat as they
traveled along?

Norbett said, "Look, I don't care if she raised and
schooled forty orphans, and brought along a tomato vine
with pineapples on it. What I want to know is—do *you*
know why she's so hell-bent on getting to California?"

In spite of Beany's resolutions, she couldn't help flar-
ing back, "It so happens that that is none of your business."

She made a grab for her belongings, tripped, and almost
lost her balance over her huaraches, which dropped as she
made her angry exit from his car. It was an ungraceful
one at best with those two elongated drums of Quaker
Oats, and the sack which she had to cradle in her arms
because of a slit that was threatening to sever it entirely.

Norbett reached out and gripped her arm, and said both
earnestly and angrily, "It so happens, Beany, that that
woman is mercenary and unscrupulous and—"

"She is not. She's going to California on a sentimental
journey."

"Sentimental, my grandmother's bustle!" he scoffed.
"She has about as much sentiment as a fox. She's stringing
you folks along with a bunch of lies."

That opening, Beany couldn't resist. Clutching her
purchases and her shoes to her, she hurled back, "You're
a fine one to talk about someone stringing someone along
with a bunch of lies. You're not so bad at that—telling me
that you—you—" But there it was again—that baseball-
sized lump which suddenly lodged in her throat. She

knew that words couldn't get past it without becoming sobs.

She turned as majestically as she could with her packages, and stalked up the steps. The package of frozen meat dropped with a plop on her toe. But she didn't stop to pick it up.

She didn't look back as she went in the door. She only heard the roar of Norbett's red car as he backed, with reckless speed, out of the driveway. But when she deposited her burdens on the kitchen table she found that she was half sobbing and finishing the unfinished sentence "—you'd meet me at the band concert unless you had to follow up a hot story. And all the time you were with *her.*"

Mary Fred had once said that there was never any peace or quiet around the Malone home for a heart to break in. Even as Beany picked up the spilled oranges and peaches with trembling hands, Martie was clutching at her skirt, asking, "Aunt Beany, help me find my gun to go in my holster." And Mary Fred was yelling from somewhere in the yard, "Bring out a package of oats, kid."

Johnny arrived with the Dodge and bellowed out blithely, "All aboard! Bring out the luggage." At the same time Miss Opal was advising, "We'd better put towels between these jars of fruit. We'll need a few towels anyway." And when Beany went out to pick up the packaged dog-meat off the top step, Johnny said, "Beany, don't forget to write an air-mail note to Elizabeth, telling her we're taking off. Tell her we're stopping at Oceanside and we'll telephone her at San Diego from there. If you hurry, Beaver, you can catch the mailman."

Beany hurried.

A furor of activity. Johnny with his usual head-in-the-clouds manner was shoving suitcases and cartons in the luggage compartment willy-nilly. Beany had to keep saying, "No—look, Johnny, this little overnight bag will fit better in here."

Mary Fred had one addition to Beany's luggage. She came out of the back door, triumphantly waving a blue can. "Here's some of your almond meal freckle-remover, Beany. Not very much—but I found it in the bathroom. Take it along. Remember, you were looking for some in a can in the kitchen cupboard one day?"

"I had two cans I used from, one upstairs and one down," Beany answered, staring at the blue can disinterestedly. "I haven't any more room in my suitcase." What difference did a few freckles, more or less, matter in Beany's life?

"I'll put it in the back of the car," Mary Fred said. "A girl should always look her best, they tell me."

A noonday sun shone hotly down when, at last, the gaping mouth of the storage compartment on the Dodge was closed; when Johnny with the help of Carlton Buell, next door, fastened the bolt on the trailer tongue and Mary Fred led Quaker up the ramp of the trailer and fastened the endgate securely; when Miss Opal settled herself in the back seat along with the folded blankets and pillows for Martie's naps, and the bucket containing the fruitful tomato vine, and a huge cretonne bag which Johnny had already labeled, "Mother's Helper," because it contained everything from iodine to needles and thread, from candy bars to toothbrushes.

"You and the forty-niners!" Mary Fred laughed, and mentioned again that her dentist made it easily in two days.

Miss Opal only said serenely, "It's nice to have your own food along and not have to depend on restaurants."

"You'll stay overnight at the Erhart ranch—and you'll just love it," Mary Fred said enviously; she had once spent a Thanksgiving vacation there with Ander. "You'll be so welcome. The minute your car stops Ander's mother and father will be out of the house and dragging you in."

Mary Fred made the first pencil marks on the map. "See, you go through Laramie and on out the highway about ten, eleven miles. Then you'll see a cattle crossing on the left and cross over—and you can't miss it."

She hugged Beany to her. She pulled Johnny's face down to her level and gave him a brother-sister peck on his cheek along with a scolding. "You should have had the haircut instead of Martie; everyone will take you for old Jim Bridger's brother." She kissed Miss Opal and the little boy, dropping a packet of gum into the pocket of his cowboy shirt. She admonished, "Just look back once in a while to see if Quaker's riding all right. But it's only a hundred and thirty-eight miles, and I don't think he'll get fidgety."

"Should we sing hymns to him if he does?" Johnny asked.

"If it should come up a hailstorm, try and pull into some shelter."

At one o'clock on Saturday, the third of July, the Malone two, plus Miss Opal, the paying passenger, plus young Martin McCallin with his gun and holster strapped on, plus a roan roping horse, the temporary passenger, drove out the Malone driveway.

They bumped out of their gateway, stopped while Johnny closed the big iron gate which was so seldom closed. Beany had to leap out to thrust back the eager Mike. Red, all adult dignity, only stood watching out of reproachful, grieving eyes.

Johnny sang as they drove north down Barberry Street, "California, here we come!" Beany, sitting beside him with the map unfolded on her lap, sang with him as heartily as she could.

Ah, the road. the beckoning road!

8

A NON-PAYING PASSENGER

The sinking sun was giving the plains a pale lavender tinge, when the Malone car and trailer stopped in a ranch driveway.

"I guess this is the Erhart place all right," Johnny said dubiously, and climbed stiffly out from the driver's seat.

"I guess it is," Beany said even more dubiously as she and Martie emerged from their side. "We crossed the cattle guard just like Mary Fred said."

There was little sign of life. No one came hurrying out from the low, rambling, part-stone, part-log ranch house to welcome them—to drag them in, as Mary Fred had predicted.

Two dogs set up an uproar of barking, but succumbed to Johnny's friendly, "Here boys!" to whisk about them curiously. In the stout corral nearby, a horse limped over to look over the top rail at them; Quaker, in his trailer, stared back superciliously. From one of the ranch buildings a calf bawled mournfully. The windmill pumped water leisurely into the watering trough beneath it.

Martie said, "Here comes a cowboy on a horse! Maybe that's Ander."

The dogs left the guests to lope out to welcome the rider. But it was not Ander, Beany realized disappointedly. Ander was taller and rode with more casual ease.

The man left his horse to drink at the watering trough and came toward them. The coil he carried in his hand was not a lasso but a coil of wire. Martie asked, "That a gun you got in your pocket?"

The broad-shouldered, short man grinned. "No, Wild Bill Hickok, just pliers and a hammer. I been out ridin' telephone poles and wires that got knocked down in a hail and windstorm."

Johnny asked, "Is this where Ander Erhart lives?"

"This is where he lives when he ain't out, tryin' to chase down his old ropin' horse." He stopped to stare at the trailer and the roan horse. "Well, I'll be a daffodil— if that don't look like Quaker in person!"

"It's Quaker, all right," Beany said. "We brought him up to Ander. When will he be home?"

The man took out the "makin's" and rolled a cigarette before he answered. "I don't reckon he'll be home for a while. He went skitin' out to California two days ago. He was feelin' pretty glum about not gettin' hold of Quaker, and one of his rodeo buddies out there wrote and told him about a horse that wasn't a bad ropin' horse that maybe he could wise up and use. So he threw his saddle in the back of his car and lit out."

Setback number one. Beany said, "Well, I guess we can just leave Quaker with Ander's folks. Would you ask his mother or father to come out?"

The ranch hand took a careful minute to lick the edge of his rolled cigarette and press the edges together, to make a twist at the end. "They ain't about either. They left yesterday mornin' for Yellowstone. They're meetin' the old man's sister there. She was to drive up from Denver —might be you know her?"

"Yes, we know her," Beany said heavily. "She lives next door to us. I saw her driving off day before yesterday."

"Fact is," the fellow resumed, "I'm holdin' down the fort myself. All the other help cleared out today to go to the big Fourth of July rodeo up near Jackson Hole tomorrow." He added enviously, "All of them aimin' to make heroes out of themselves."

Martie contributed, "I got a gun."

The man looked down at the little boy and said, "Looks like you got a jaw full of chewin' tobacco, too."

"Oh, my goodness!" Miss Opal said. "He's got that whole pack of gum in his mouth."

"I chewed it all up because I was hungry," the child stated.

"Burt's my name," the man said. "You pile out and come on in. Got plenty to eat. Plenty of beds. I'd have supper ready, only it took me longer to get those wires patched up and pounded into place than I figured on. Ought to be able to get calls through now, though."

Beany thought then, as she was to think many times afterward, how differently events might have turned out if Burt had only put those telephone wires in working order two days before. Then Mary Fred could have reached Ander before he went skitin' out to California. Then the Malones would have been minus a roping horse and plus the money she and Johnny had paid for the trailer.

Miss Opal said briskly, "Now, Burt, you just show me where things are in the kitchen and I'll tend to getting supper. You take care of the horse. None of us knows much about horses."

That, of course, was a slight understatement. Miss Opal, as well as Beany, was frightened of horses. "I keep thinking how just one foot is big enough to kick your whole face in," she had confessed to Beany. Whereas Johnny had no fear of them, he had only the vaguest idea about a horse's care, diet, or whims.

Beany said, "I guess it will be all right just to leave Quaker with you until Ander comes home. It's the only thing we can do."

She took Martie's hand and walked toward the ranch house with a great feeling of relief to see Burt moving confidently toward the endgate of the trailer. Thus must the Ancient Mariner have felt when the albatross finally dropped.

Miss Opal filled in the supper menu of fried ham and boiled potatoes, which Burt would have cooked for himself, with her fried chicken, rolls, and canned peaches. Miss Opal tidied up the kitchen afterwards while Beany unpacked Martie's sleepers and put him to bed.

Beany was alone in the ranch house the next morning when the telephone rang. Johnny had gone out with Burt

and Martie to see a new colt. Miss Opal was repacking the
back seat of the car, and checking to see if her canned fruit
had ridden safely.

Beany wasn't sure whether that telephone ring, two
hearty longs and a short, was for the Erhart ranch or not.
Gingerly she took the receiver from the wall telephone
and held it to her ear.

A hum of wires like a multitude of bees and through it
a man's voice repeating, "Hello—hello," and an operator's distant voice saying, "La Jolla, California, calling.
Here is your party." In answer to Beany's small, dubious,
"Hello," the man's voice asked, "This you, Mother?"

It was Ander.

"No. No, your mother went to Yellowstone, Ander.
This is Beany Malone. We came up—"

"Beany Malone, what are you doing on the ranch? Mary
Fred there?"

"No. Mary Fred had to go back to her dude ranch.
We're on our way to California. Ander, Mary Fred found
Quaker for you and we brought him up to you but—"

"Quaker!" Beany wished Mary Fred's ear, rather than
hers, could have heard his low shout of amazement and
joy, his almost incoherent, "No kidding? Old Quaker
himself? Just when I'd abandoned hope of ever seeing the
old rascal again. You're sure it's Quaker? Has he got the
Lazy E on his left hip, and a blurry upside-down seven in
his forehead?"

"Yes—and he even followed Mary Fred with a box of
Quaker Oats."

"That's him! That's the old boy, all right. Why, Beany,
with that horse under me and a rope in my hand, I can
clean up five—maybe six hundred dollars in prize money.

You say you brought him up in a trailer? Does it ride pretty smooth? Is it a well-built trailer?"

"Yes, it is—the man built it himself and we—"

"What route are you taking out?"

"The northern. We'll stop at Oceanside first because—"

"Beany, couldn't you bring Quaker with you? You won't be more than a couple or three days on the road—"

"We have to stop at Fort Bridger for Johnny to check up on data on old Jim Bridger."

"Even so, three or four days. I made it out in two. I could meet you at Oceanside. I can't take time to come back because I have to pay my entrance fees at all these fairs and rodeos I'll be entering. Beany, I can't tell you what a favor it would be. You wouldn't mind bringing him along, would you?"

Beany wanted to shout it loud. "Yes, yes, we would mind. This is supposed to be a vacation trip for me. And I don't like horses—even special horses named Quaker— and they don't like me." But after all she was a Malone. Ander was their friend. Ander had done many favors for them. So she found herself saying, though not too heartily, "Well—I guess—we could."

The operator at Ander's end cut in with her, "Your three minutes is up." She could hear Ander saying, "Don't cut me off. Hold everything till I drop some more money in." She heard the repeated ping of silver coins as Ander dropped them in the slots.

"Listen, Beany," he said, "I'll be watching for you at Oceanside. As you come into the town there are a lot of motels and you stop at the second—it might be the third one. It's got a lot of trees around it, and it's trimmed in blue—you can't miss it. The folks that run it are real nice and they—"

"What'll we feed the horse—and how much?" Beany broke in anxiously.

"What have you been giving him?"

"Mary Fred could only get cracked corn at a chicken-feed store and she said he didn't like it."

"Give him oats. Give him a gallon measure full, night and morning. No grain at noon as long as he isn't working. Don't let him drink too heavy if he's hot. And, Beany, could you take a bale of alfalfa from the ranch? He's an alfalfa-hay horse, and it'll keep him in good flesh. Is he in pretty good shape?"

"Yes, Mary Fred said he was beautiful."

"That's perfect. Beany, do you suppose you could exercise him a little, mornings and evenings, on the trek out? Just so he won't get stove up?"

The operator cut in again with her reminder that another three minutes was up and Ander's voice said in parting, "I'll be watching for you, Beany, and you'll never know how much—" The connection was abruptly cut off.

Beany backed away from the wall telephone and sat down limply. A gallon measure of oats night and morning. Quaker was an alfalfa-hay horse. Not too much water when he was hot. And could they exercise him? Now that was asking too much.

And then a chill thought struck Beany and she left the chair in sudden panic. She hadn't remembered to tell Ander about the farmer who was counting the days off—

four days only!—before he would come to the Malone
home for his money *or* his horse. And he would find the
horse gone. His grim parting words had been, "He's got
to stay right here till he's paid for." Oh, why hadn't she
thought to give Ander the man's name and tell him to
rush the money to him from California?

She tried to call him back. She jiggled the receiver hook
up and down but got no response. She turned the crank
long and furiously until the local operator answered
chidingly, "You don't have to ring that long." Beany gave
frantic explanation about the call from California and
ended pleadingly, "I've *got* to talk to him some more."

The operator was sympathetic but helpless. "There's
no way we can trace a call from a pay station, honey."

Johnny, the optimist, was not troubled by Beany's for-
getfulness in telling Ander about the financial angle of
Quaker, nor was he daunted by the burden of a trailer
full of horse behind their car. "It'll be all right. Quaker
won't slow us down any. We ought to check in at Oceanside in three, maybe four days at the most, and Ander can
shoot a letter right back to the farmer—what was his
name now?"

"Oliver Hart. But he said he'd come in Monday—and
this is Sunday already."

"I imagine Oliver Hart will have a heart and know our
intentions are good. Ander can even wire the money to
him. Don't worry about it, little Beaver. This is your
vacation."

Yes, it was her vacation and she was going to California.
Beany's spirits lifted. The Wyoming wind cooled, even
as a hot sun beat down. Again they loaded in suitcases and

cartons. Beany even learned how to let down the endgate for Quaker to march up and into the trailer.

Burt helped Johnny wire on a bale of alfalfa between the fender and hood of the car. On the other side Johnny fitted a bedroll. "It's Ander's," he explained. "Might have some use for it on the way out. If they charge too much for cottage camps, we'll just get a one-room affair for you womenfolks and I'll bed down in this."

They said good-by to Burt, who had a going-away present for Miss Opal. A dozen boiled eggs. "Eggs are just pilin' up on me," he said, "with all the folks gone. Might be handy to have along."

His tanned face reddened happily under Miss Opal's thanks. Miss Opal had a genius for leaving people happier than she found them. "You folks be sure to stop in on your way back," he invited heartily. He found a gallon measure and gave it to them to facilitate the feeding of Quaker. He added, "Now you can make it to Evanston—that's a little ways on the other side of Fort Bridger—easy as pie by sundown. Just hug old Highway 30 all the way."

Highway 30, wide and ribbon smooth! Beany and Johnny spelled each other driving. It seemed only natural to sing an accompaniment to the whir of the motor and hum of tires. Beany thought, New places, new faces—they do make you forget. Almost. She thought ahead to seeing Elizabeth and Don; and that nice young man Elizabeth would find for her. Good-by, Norbett, it's been nice knowing you—Hah!

They drew off the road and ate lunch under a cotton-wood tree beside a sand creek. Hard-boiled eggs, rolls, and Miss Opal's tomatoes. "Nooning, the old-timers called it," Johnny said. "I keep thinking of those old fellows, crawling along in their covered wagons, watching out for Indians, praying for water for their horses and oxen. Do you suppose we ought to water our livestock?"

"Couldn't we just give him some in a bucket without taking him out of the trailer?" Beany suggested.

"No, we ought to limber him up a little," Johnny said. "He must get as stiff and cramped, standing up there, as we do sitting in the car."

It took longer than it should—for they were amateurs at it—to let down the endgate, back Quaker down it. The tomato plant in the bucket held great fascination for him. Miss Opal had to put it back in the car. Quaker nibbled the grass and young sunflowers, pulling Johnny along with him. It was hard going to get him back into the trailer.

They didn't make it to Evanston by sundown. They made it instead to a small Wyoming town on the near side of Fort Bridger. And they didn't make it easy as pie. For on this Fourth of July holiday all of Colorado, Utah, and Wyoming seemed to have taken to the road.

The little towns they passed through were so packed with cars and people that they had to weave their way with slow care. Firecrackers popped here and there, and one celebrant even threw one in Quaker's trailer. He reared and plunged in such fright that he knocked a board loose. Beany, driving, stopped outside the town and Johnny got out and pounded it back as best he could, using a tire tool for a hammer.

The trailer hampered their speed. It had a tendency to whiplash back and forth if, on a smooth stretch, they went over forty-five. "Oh gosh!" Beany breathed once in fright, when an eager driver cut around another car and, passing them closely, missed grazing the lurching trailer by a bare quarter-inch. So they drove, watching the speedometer, watching behind to see that Quaker was riding smoothly, not rocking.

Because of the wired-on bale of hay, they couldn't open the driver's door. Twice they had to stop to fasten the bedroll more securely. And little Martie had all the wants of an almost five-year-old. He was hungry, he was thirsty, or he'd fidget uncomfortably and announce, "When are we going to get to a bathroom?" Mary Fred's dentist, decided Beany ruefully, couldn't have been dragging a horse in a trailer with his rations wired on, or have had for a passenger a small boy, when he covered the road from Denver to Salt Lake in one sunup to sundown.

They reached the Wyoming town a few miles from Fort Bridger at dusk. They were hot, tired, and hungry. They stopped at three cottage camps only to be met by a "No Vacancy" sign.

"All the world is on the wing this Fourth of July week end," Johnny sighed as he drove on to another.

Beany got out and walked toward the office just as a tired and harassed woman turned the sign, which said "Vacancy" on one side, around to read, "No Vacancy." Beany queried, "Wouldn't you have room for us to stay here tonight?"

"No, I wouldn't," she answered sharply. "I've had people coming and going this whole day. Everything's full up. The whole town is, as far as I know."

Beany walked back to the car. New places, new faces

could also mean strange places, strange faces. She had never felt this feeling of being a stranger in a strange land before.

She reported despairingly to the ones in the car, "There isn't any room here either."

Miss Opal straightened the wide, wilted velvet belt, the buckle of which had worked far to the side. "Let me go talk to her."

She was in the office a long time. She came out with a key and the heartening announcement, "She'll let us have that one at the far end. She said the people just moved out of it and the beds aren't made, but I told her I'd make them and we didn't care whether the sheets were ironed or not. As soon as we have supper, I told her I'd help her get the bedding that she washed this morning off the line. Yes, and I asked her to eat supper with us—the poor thing's been so busy all day she hasn't had time to fix herself a bite. We've got plenty."

Johnny murmured to Beany, "I guess Miss Opal never met a stranger in her life."

Gratefully, wearily the travelers took over the boxy room with its two beds. The cottage-camp owner brought over sheets and a pitcher of fresh milk. "I figured the little fellow would need it." Miss Opal asked her, "Which would you rather have for supper—coffee or tea? We've got both."

"Coffee. I've been dying for a cup of coffee for hours." She went hurrying back to the office to explain to a carload of travelers that her "No Vacancy" sign meant just that.

Miss Opal set about to fix supper. She said to Johnny,

"This woman, Mattie Leavitt is her name, has lived here for forty years. Her father-in-law was one of the early settlers. Might be she could tell you who to talk to about this old pioneer—what was his name now?"

"Jim Bridger."

"Uh-huh. Mattie's a nice, friendly person. She'll help you."

"Miss Opal, you're wonderful," Johnny said. "You're perfect for running interference."

Yes, wonderful, Beany thought, Miss Opal, extending neighborly friendliness, had found it. Gone was the stranger-in-a-strange-land feeling. The little room already had a homey welcome for them.

9

ENTER CYNTHIA

It was late afternoon of the next day when Beany left
Johnny and the car at a garage on the main street of the
little town and walked the short distance out to their
cottage camp at the edge of town.

Johnny had spent a long and full day at Fort Bridger.
To Beany it was only a clump of old buildings in a setting of tall grass, ancient cottonwoods, and pine trees, with
a stone wall surrounding it. But Johnny's historical mind
could look at the old Pony Express stables and visualize
a lathered pony being led through the door by a rider
with a wind-bitten face and clothes chalky with dust.

Johnny could look at the traps in the museum and, in
imagination, trudged along through crusted snow with
cunning old trappers to check them. Johnny's mind
peopled the grove with whiskered, heavy-booted men with
long rifles ever close at hand. Beany marveled at, even

envied, Johnny's faculty of losing himself in the past. It would be a pleasant retreat when the present jarred unpleasantly.

Johnny took pictures. He followed up leads which Mattie Leavitt, cottage-camp owner, gave him. One old lady told him her brother owned a memorandum Jim Bridger had given their father regarding the purchase of beef cattle for the fort. She promised, "I'll get it for you and have it ready when you come back this way from California."

Johnny stayed on at the garage to have a mechanic ease the brakes, which Mac, in tightening up the car, had given too quick and decisive a grip. Johnny would also have the tank filled and the oil checked so that they could make an early start in the morning.

Miss Opal had just returned to their room at the cottage camp and had slipped off her shoes to ease her swollen feet. She had been helping her new friend, Mattie, freshen up the cabins. Beany asked, "Did Martie get along all right while Johnny and I were gone?"

Oh yes, indeed, Miss Opal reported, he had been a lamb, playing about all day.

There was Quaker to be cared for.

Beany filled the gallon measure out of the fifty-pound sack of oats they had bought last evening. It was amazing how a sack of oats dwindled when you scooped it out, a gallon at a time. "But, Beany," Johnny had reasoned, "if you weighed twelve hundred pounds you, too, would put away a gallon at one sitting—or standing."

She carried it to where Quaker was staked in a field at the edge of the cottage courts. This, too, was a favor granted by Mattie. Usually Quaker gave an eager nicker and attacked his meal with relish. But not this evening. He only looked at Beany out of apathetic eyes, and didn't move.

She filled his bucket with fresh water, sloshed it about enticingly. "Don't you want a cold drink, Quaker?" But still he stood, legs slightly spread, head hanging heavily. Perhaps it was the heat, Beany told herself.

She spoke to Miss Opal about it when she returned to their quarters. "Did you ever have a horse on your little truck farm, Miss Opal?"

"No, pet, I never raised anything bigger than a turkey."

"You don't suppose Quaker could be sick, do you?" Beany pursued worriedly. "He's just standing out there, drooping."

"Maybe it's the heat," Miss Opal comforted. "It's been terrible hot. But there's a breeze stirring now to cool things off."

And then Johnny came in. He was carrying a square-shaped old lantern, and rubbing at a spot of rust on it with his handkerchief. "Look at this old relic! Got to talking to a fellow who works at the garage and he gave it to me. Look at the wick. Nothing but a piece of cloth pulled through a button, so the oil wouldn't flare up when it was lighted. They evidently burned snake or skunk oil in these, because though coal oil was shipped in in the sixties, I doubt if the plainsmen could get it."

"I'd rather have a flashlight," Beany said practically. "Is the car all ready for taking off in the morning?"

"Rearin' to go," Johnny said. "And guess what? I've got another passenger to take with us to California."

"Another passenger!" Beany said. "But my gosh, Johnny, we're pretty crowded as it is."

"She said she wouldn't mind riding in the back seat with Miss Opal—"

"Oh, it's a *she*! How old?"

"Maybe about your age, Beany. It was like this. When I was in the garage, she came up to me and asked me if we were going to California. She said she was on her way out, but that she had to turn out for a big truck on the road, and she ran into a ditch and broke her axle. And she just *has* to get to California."

"Now that'll be nice," Miss Opal said. "If the poor thing had a breakdown and has to get there, we can make room for her."

"And it'll be nice for us," Johnny said happily, "because she's like Mary Fred—she vibrates to horses. She rides in horse shows. All these puzzling equine vagaries are an open book to her."

"Where is she?" Beany asked.

"She's here. I showed her Quaker and she's out communing with him." He lowered his voice to say, "Beany, I—well, I didn't talk money with her. She said she'd gladly pay her way. So I thought you—that you—"

"I know," Beany sighed. "You thought I could do the dirty work, as per usual."

"I'm sure anything you say would be all right with her," Johnny said largely. He broke off as the doorway was darkened, and turned to the newcomer. "Here we are, Cynthia—come on in. This is my sister, Beany, and Miss Opal, and the little fellow perusing—in his own peculiar, preschool fashion—the Bugs Bunny comic is little Martie, sometimes known as Big Ears. Cynthia—the last name is Hobbs, you said?"

"That's right, Hobbs," a cool voice said.

Beany stared at the new girl, and all her mistrust and dislike showed in her honest, amazed face. Even when Johnny repeated, "Beany, this is Cynthia," she couldn't muster a "Hello, Cynthia," much less a, "We're glad you're going with us." Cynthia! The girl of the white dress who had sat across the table from Norbett Rhodes in the Ragged Robin. The girl who was responsible for Beany's misery, her lost illusions about men—no, just one man.

Cynthia wasn't wearing a white sunback dress now with gold belt and sandals, but a full, green cotton skirt with pockets big as mail pouches, with a matching crew shirt with diagonal stripes of rose, lavender, and the apple green of the skirt. Her sandals, Beany noted, had the same pastel shades and part of Beany's mind was thinking irrelevantly, I can never match things that perfectly. But then I don't shop at exclusive stores.

The girl's voice broke into Beany's unhappy thoughts. "Your horse has colic. Didn't you notice that he didn't eat anything? He hasn't touched the grain you put out for him."

Beany stammered, "I know he didn't—but I thought maybe he just wasn't hungry then."

Martie looked up from page eleven of Bugs Bunny. "He was hungry today," he said. "I fed him."

"What did you feed him?" Johnny, Beany, and Cynthia asked him almost in unison.

"He liked them," the little boy said. "He ate them right

out of my hand—a whole lot of tomatoes. All kinds of them. He liked the little-bitty green ones."

"Oh dear!" Miss Opal said. "He was playing around while I helped Mattie. I looked out every now and then and saw him climbing in and out of the car, but I had no idea— Let me look at my tomato plant. Maybe the poor, innocent lamb didn't give him many."

But he had. The tomato vine with its generous flowering of red and green was almost denuded.

"Maybe we ought to get a vet," Beany said faintly.

"I know what to do for colic," the girl said. "I used to have a horse that got it. He was crazy about apples and used to poke his head through the fence into the orchard and eat too many. Warm salt water, all we can pour down him, will fix him up, I'm sure."

Beany and Miss Opal fixed the warm salt water. Cynthia and Johnny, aided by a boy from the cottage camp filling station, poured it down his protesting throat from a ginger ale bottle. Cynthia did have a loving but firm manner with a horse. She patted him encouragingly, she scolded him, she kept him walking about.

For an hour the little group, with Cynthia giving orders, worked over and watched the roan horse anxiously. Then, much to their delight, he perked up in horse fashion. His ears pricked forward as a train whistled; he switched his tail indignantly at flies. He even walked over to a succulent spot of weeds and started nibbling.

"Cynthia," Johnny said admiringly, "I don't know what we'd have done without you. You're elected valet to Quaker." He turned to Beany and Miss Opal. "Isn't she miraculous?"

Miss Opal assented whole-heartedly. Beany said nothing.

And now Johnny, his mind relieved about Quaker, had plans. "You know what would be fun," he said with that highlighted enthusiasm which was so contagious. "Let's have a picnic supper out at the Fort Bridger grounds. A lot of folks picnicked there today but I imagine it will be deserted tonight. I'll take along my lantern and we can just imagine that we are old-timers camping out there on our way to 'Californy.' "

Miss Opal, ever amiable, ever amenable, said readily, "Now that would be nice. Nicer than eating in this stuffy room. We still have fried chicken and rolls. You girls get yourselves ready and I'll see to the food."

The two girls found themselves alone in the room.

Cynthia changed out of her silken T shirt and the full, green skirt on which salt water had splashed while she worked with Quaker. Beany watched with grudging admiration as she pulled on, as she fastened the narrow belt of, a sleeveless gingham of dusty pink and gray plaid. She tied a narrow pink scarf around her dark, smoky hair.

Beany rummaged through her suitcase. Not the white dress. She wondered if she would ever be satisfied with that dress again. It was such a cheap edition of the one Cynthia had worn that fateful night in Beany's life. Not the green-striped seersucker. Though the store ad, which had enticed Beany, had read, "Spare the iron without spoiling the dress. It will come out of the suds fresh as a daisy," the collar looked more rumpled than any daisy ought to look. Beany was angry with herself that she was even trying to compete with Cynthia, who had preëmpted the mirror over the dresser. You'd think she'd move over and give somebody else room to look at herself.

Hastily Beany grabbed out of her suitcase her overall-blue denim skirt and a red-checked blouse. She caught a glimpse of Cynthia's dark eyes in the mirror as Cynthia painstakingly, lovingly smoothed dark powder on her tanned skin. And again Beany felt anger quicken her pulses. The girl looked so proud of herself, so pleased with herself.

Beany burst out, "We're going to be crowded in our car. If you wanted to get to California, why didn't you take the bus? You'd make good time on it."

The girl didn't turn to look at Beany, but kept right on smoothing powder over and under her chin. "I don't like buses," she said. "I thought it would be nicer to go with some folks who are going direct to Oceanside. And Johnny," she added with a malicious fleck of triumph in her smile, "thought it would be nice for you to have company your own age. Evidently you don't share his enthusiasm."

Beany answered honestly as she tucked in the tail of her shirt without benefit of mirror, "No, I don't." She added, "Johnny told me that you'd be willing to pay for going out with us. Is—is twenty-five dollars all right with you?"

"Perfectly all right," was the casual answer. "Only you'll have to wait till I get to Oceanside to get it."

"But supposing we need it? We might run pretty close on buying gas and oil, and for cottage camps and—well, all expenses."

"Your gas and oil, or your cottage camps won't cost any more with me along."

She turned from the mirror then to walk over to her overnight bag for further make-up. She looked at Beany and for an instant her brown arrogant eyes locked with Beany's angry gray ones. "I don't care whether you want me along or not. I'm used to girls' not liking me. I have never liked other girls either."

Beany was about to hurl back, "Have you ever liked anyone beside yourself?" when Miss Opal came into the room. She dropped down on the bed, panting noticeably as she always did after any exertion, and said admiringly, "You girls look real pretty. I suppose I ought to put on a fresh lace collar but, my goodness, it'll soon be dark. That red blouse is pretty on you, Beany, with your red cheeks. I like red."

"Is that why you wear a red belt with a lavender flowered dress?" Cynthia asked pointedly—insultingly, it seemed to Beany.

"That's one reason," Miss Opal said comfortably. She got to her feet then and said, "We can take coffee in the thermos jug. Beany, love, look there in that carton at the foot of the bed, and get some paper napkins and cups. Oh yes, and salt. We'll need salt for the tomatoes."

Cynthia said, "I thought the little boy took care of the tomatoes for you."

"There're a few left," Miss Opal said. "Enough for our picnic supper tonight. And then," she added regretfully, "I guess there's no use taking the plant along with us. But, at least, it'll give us more room in the back seat."

Cynthia laughed deridingly. "We certainly would have looked like Okies with a tomato plant riding along with us."

"It isn't how we look, it's getting there that counts," Miss Opal said unruffled.

Cynthia, giving a last touch to her full lips with a dark, purplish lipstick, said only, "I'm ready," and walked out to where Johnny puttered about the car, leaving Beany and Miss Opal to worry about paper napkins, salt, and making coffee to fill the thermos jug.

Beany burst out, "I wish—I just wish that crazy Johnny hadn't foisted that girl off on us. I don't like her. Johnny's thinking she's miraculous!"

Miss Opal said matter-of-factly, "I feel sorry for her."

"You feel sorry for *her!*" Beany exclaimed. "Why would anyone feel sorry for her? If you want to feel sorry for someone, feel sorry for me—yes, and you, too—for having to put up with her high-handed airs and graces. She certainly isn't the kind to brighten the corner where she is."

"She isn't happy," Miss Opal said slowly. "Disagreeable people seldom are. The poor child is empty inside. She hasn't had happiness and faith around her the way you have." She reached over and patted Beany's stiff back. "I couldn't feel sorry for you, child, any more than I could for myself. Life has been good to us. . . . Should I put cream right in with the coffee? And we'd better take a sweater for the little fellow for the night's chill."

10

"YOU TELL ME YOUR DREAM—"

Beany was to receive one more jolt this day. One which sent her heart thudding up in her throat, and momentarily drained the flushed color from her face until the freckles stood out in bold formation across her nose.

Miss Opal and Beany were loading the back seat with blankets, pillows, sweaters, thermos jug, and rearranging the picnic food to make room for the three who must sit in the back. For Cynthia sat in state in the front seat and, even though Miss Opal was saying, "It'll be more crowded going out than coming home, because we won't have so much to bring back," Cynthia never offered, "Martie can sit up here in front."

Johnny, Cynthia informed them, was making the rounds of the cottage camp to see if he could find some oil that would burn in his old Jim Bridger lantern. Martie, kneeling on top of a carton in the back seat, was looking out the back window when he yelled out joyously, "Here comes Johnny—and look!—*he's* with him. Oh goody!" He immediately made a scrambling exodus, tumbling the folded blankets to the floor, and ran to meet Johnny and the *he* who accompanied him.

That's when Beany looked up, clutching paper napkins and the salt shaker, and her heart began acting like something else besides an organ for pumping blood through her veins. For the *he* was Norbett Rhodes. His thin face was burned from driving in Wyoming's wind and sun. He was pretending great interest in the workings of the wick in Johnny's lantern.

It was such a noisy, confused meeting, and for that Beany was thankful. Surely no one would notice that her shaking hands were letting the salt spill out of the shaker onto the paper napkins she clutched. Not when Martie was capering about and shouting, "He brought me caps for my gun. And I know how to tear off a little teeny-weeny piece like this, and put it in."

Not when Johnny was announcing happily, "Look what I found when I went hunting for skunk oil. Now there's devotion for you—a guy that burns up the road through half of Colorado and almost all of Wyoming to catch up with Beany Malone."

Norbett was fumbling for something in his pocket. He brought out two pairs of dark glasses and, trying hard to be self-contained and casual, said, "You dropped these, Beany, in my car that day we—I mean, that morning you left, and I—well, I've got some newspaper business that might take me to California and I—I just thought I might run into you folks—"

Beany stammered honestly, "I forgot—I ever bought those dark glasses."

"We're going on a picnic supper out at Fort Bridger," Johnny interrupted heartily. "Your timing was perfect, Norbett, for getting in on the party. Miss Opal, we've got plenty for one more, haven't we?"

Miss Opal was backing out of the car after refolding the blankets Martie had tumbled. "Full and plenty," she answered, beaming at both Beany and the boy she assumed to be Beany's boy friend. "It's fine that you got here in time to go with us."

Beany said, "This is Miss Opal, Norbett. . . ." Does she look like an old witch? You said she was mercenary and unscrupulous. . . .

Johnny was saying, "And, Norbett, this is Cynthia Hobbs, our latest acquisition." Beany waited tensely for Norbett's answer. He only muttered, "Yeh, I've seen Cynthia about. Her father lives at the Park Gate, where I do." Cynthia, herself, who had been sitting with a sphinx-like smile on her face, only nodded and said brightly, "Fancy meeting you here!"

I've seen Cynthia about! Fancy meeting you here! What particular brand of wool were those two trying to pull over folks' eyes? Or, more specifically, over Beany's, for no one would have to *try* to pull wool over the trusting eyes of Johnny or Miss Opal.

Ah, but Cynthia was fast on her feet when it came to getting things the way Cynthia wanted them. Not that Beany *wanted* Norbett to sit on the crowded back seat with her. Still, she couldn't help noticing the smooth way that Cynthia moved over closer to Johnny as he slid in behind the wheel, how she pulled her full plaid skirts about her and murmured, "Better sit up here, Norbett, so you won't squash a hard-boiled egg or a tomato." That left the ample Miss Opal, the squirming Martie, the food-stuffs, and a seething Beany in the back seat.

Beany kept on seething. They came to an intersection where a roadside stand sold watermelons, and Cynthia exclaimed, "Oh, watermelon! I love watermelon on a picnic." Johnny, the generous, immediately pulled up at the side of the road and drew out of their scanty traveling funds a bill and some silver in exchange for a long water-melon which had to lie on Beany's feet the rest of the way.

The trees at the now deserted Fort Bridger cast long shadows as the six spread blankets and lugged cartons from the car. As five did, rather, for Cynthia only watched in what Beany labeled her "Lady Castlemaine" air. Again Cynthia deftly maneuvered the seating arrangement so that Cynthia sat between Johnny and Norbett. Not that Beany *wanted t*o sit next to Norbett!

There were so many things for Beany to seethe over. Miss Opal's pressing the white meat of the chicken on Cynthia and Norbett while she, the true hostess, con-tented herself with a back and neck. They had forgotten to put in an extra paper cup after Norbett's arrival. Didn't Norbett even notice that Miss Opal relinquished her cup of coffee to him? She went without coffee until Martie finished his milk, and then quietly took over his cup. All this, after Norbett's maligning her, saying she had no more sentiment than a fox.

Cynthia ate only a little of the heart of her slice of

watermelon—the watermelon she had insisted on, even though they had enough food without it.

When the last of the coffee gurgled out of the thermos jug, Miss Opal said out of her old-maid, matchmaking instinct, "Now, Martie and I can clear things up here. Maybe you young folks would like to stroll around the grounds before it gets too dark."

Johnny had been sitting quietly, his long legs outstretched, his arms behind him acting as props to his slanted top. His face was turned upward to the darkening sky with an absorbed dreaminess. He roused and said, "You know what would be nice? Because you know what our sitting here in a circle reminds me of? Way back in the late forties a group of six assorted people met here. They were all taking the Oregon trail west. And they all sat around a fire—maybe right here in this spot. I'll bet they had a lantern with the wick sputtering in skunk oil, just like this one is—"

"What *have* you got in it?" Beany asked. "It smells like frying fish."

"Some grease that Mattie poured out of her skillet," Johnny answered. "And so those travelers back in the past sat around, and each one told why he or she was going to California. Each one sort of opened his heart and showed the pull or the push behind his going. I read about it in one of the old journals. One conceited dope wanted to get rich so he could have a diamond setting in a front tooth. One woman wanted a home with a bay window where she could hang a canary—in a cage, that is—and grow geraniums in tin cans. One, a preacher, was risking his scalp so as to go to the gold diggings and save souls. I couldn't help thinking when I read it how folks could be together, doing the thises and thatses of everyday living, but that it's so much more interesting to know what's inside that makes them tick."

"That's right," Miss Opal encouraged. "You tell us, Johnny, why you're taking this trip."

"You tell me your dream, Johnny," Cynthia said flippantly, "and I'll tell you mine."

Couldn't Johnny detect the mockery in her voice? Evidently not. For Johnny's warm smile enveloped them all. Johnny's smile, Beany thought, was brighter than the panting, feeble light of the lantern he was nursing so hopefully.

"Well, I guess most of you know that I started out to do a little more tracking down of old Jim Bridger. Maybe it bores you to hear about it and, by golly, I wouldn't blame you. But when I dig around in the lives of the old codgers who—to use a moth-eaten phrase—shaped the West, I get a big kick to find out how human they were. Sure, they had courage and stubbornness but they, too, nursed grudges, they were full of conceit and vainglory. Like old Jim Bridger telling those tall tales about Yellowstone Park—"

"They weren't such tall tales after all," Norbett put in. "Go on, Johnny."

"So when the history prof out at the U said he'd like me to work on his folklore series—"

Norbett interrupted again. "No other college freshman was ever given that much recognition, I'll have you know. It's nice to see genius recognized."

"—and for my stint gave me old Jim Bridger to dig out

of the dust—well, I felt a little like Lancelot going after the Holy Grail—"

"I thought it was King Arthur," Beany murmured.

"You get paid for it, don't you?" Cynthia asked.

"Yes—my tuition, which is quite a boost. In a family like ours you have to boost yourself along. It keeps poor old Pop strapped, as it is, buying groceries for someone with an appetite like mine. Seems almost too good to be true that I can get my tuition for doing something that's such fun to do. Maybe I'll be able to dig up some more data in California libraries while Beany is having herself a fling. So that's it, folks. Thank you for your kind attention and may I introduce the next speaker, Cynthia Hobbs. Step right up to the mike, Cynthia, and tell us why you are going to California."

Cynthia answered promptly, "I could tell you in three little words, *to get money*. I've been waiting for it ever since I was old enough to know anything, and now—" Did Beany imagine it, or did Norbett, sitting next to Cynthia, give her a warning nudge?

Miss Opal asked, "What do you want money for, child?"

"What does anybody want money for?" she flung back as though the questioner was foolish even to ask it. "Because I'm a spoiled brat and I want more things than I've got."

Miss Opal pursued, "But you have parents, don't you?"

"Do I! I have the maximum of parents, you might say. Two mothers and two fathers. My mother and father were divorced when I was eleven."

"Oh dear!" Miss Opal breathed.

"But I suppose you live with your mother, don't you?" Johnny asked.

"No, they divide me evenly—or unevenly. I live with my mother and her husband in Laramie during the school term, and with my father and his wife at the Park Gate Hotel in summer."

"Oh, that's too bad," Miss Opal broke out.

"It has its advantages," Cynthia said coolly. "It gets to be quite a game—playing one set of parents against the other. Even though neither couple is *too* crazy about having you with them, cluttering up their lives, yet they don't like the idea of your being fonder of or partial to the others. It didn't take me long to learn the gentle art of chiseling. It's amazing how much you can get out of them —luxury items, that is, as well as going places and doing things. All I have to do is say to Mother and Paul—he's her husband— 'But Father and Irene let me drive *their* car,' and so, in order not to be outdone, they let me take theirs. And when I'm with Father, I can always needle him by saying, 'But Mother and Paul always give me money to get—' well, whatever I've set my little heart on. I started as a kid getting shoe skates and bicycles—always better shoe skates and bicycles than other kids my age. And in high school I always got fur coats and wrist watches and opera tickets."

"Are you through high school?" Johnny asked.

"Yes, I finished last June. I'm going back east to college."

"Well, from now on you won't have to stoop to that sort of chiseling," Johnny commiserated. "Because you can get some sort of a job to boost you along. I tell you what you could do, as long as you have a miraculous touch with horses. You could do what our Mary Fred does. She goes out to the riding stables every Saturday and teaches little kids how to ride."

"And she works at a dude ranch in the summer," Beany added.

"I'm not teaching kids how to ride. And I'm not wet-nursing a bunch of snobbish dudes in the summer," she said shortly. "I'm going to major in music at college and be a concert singer."

You would, Beany thought. You'd want to stand in front of an audience with the spotlight on you.

Young Martie had settled himself on Miss Opal's lap. He lifted his head to ask, "Is the money in a great big pile out in California? A great big pile?"

Again Beany had the feeling that in the dark Norbett nudged Cynthia warningly. Cynthia answered vaguely, "It's there. I'll tell you about it after I get it. So ends Cynthia's confession story," she added with a short, almost defiant laugh.

"You're next, Norbett," Johnny said, breaking the queer, shocked silence that fell on the small circle.

Norbett only sat, plucking at the grass nervously, and Johnny prompted him, "Tell us about your dream of being a hot-shot newspaper man. Bare all, so that when you get famous I can do one of those personal stories and call it, 'The Man I Knew.' "

Norbett seemed to pick up Cynthia's challenging defiance. For he gave a harsh, grunting laugh and said, "You could lead off your story, Johnny, by saying, 'Norbett Rhodes was always a show-off.' "

Miss Opal cluck-clucked discountingly, "Oh no, you're not. I've always been one to size up a person's character by his face. I could tell the minute I looked at you that you'd be dependable and kind and always do what you thought was right. Maybe you make mistakes, but you'd be the kind to admit them."

You see only good in people, Beany thought. You even think I'm good, but I'm not. I'm mean and hateful and jealous.

Norbett's voice softened to somewhat the same honest sincerity of Johnny's. "I've always wanted people to notice me—to think I was wonderful. I guess I've always craved a pat on the head—just like that silly pup, Mike, at the Malones'. Like once, after my folks died, and my aunt and uncle had to take me to live with them at the Park Gate. I sensed of course that I was just a cross they had to put up with. And I did all sorts of dumb things, hoping to make them like me. The very first money I made, throwing dodgers around at doors, I bought my aunt a silver necklace. It was heavy as a dog chain, but somehow I thought it was beautiful—"

It was as though a clenched hand squeezed at Beany's heart. Don't say any more about the necklace, Norbett, she begged inwardly. A scene flashed through her mind. Of a heavy silver necklace dropping out of Norbett's pocket one day when he took out his car keys, of Norbett's mumbling, "Guess I ought to toss that thing in the trash can where it belongs." And he had told Beany of giving it to his aunt years before, how she never wore it, how he had found it in some castoffs she was giving to the Salvation Army.

Beany had said promptly, "I think it's beautiful. If it was shortened a little, it would make a perfect charm bracelet." So on Christmas morning the present that gladdened Beany's heart more than any other had been a charm bracelet with two charms already attached. A miniature car, which was a reasonable facsimile of the low-slung car Norbett drove, a miniature bottle which Norbett said contained freckle cream.

She was suddenly glad that she hadn't thrown the bracelet in the ashpit, glad that Mary Fred had made her promise to wear it until she was sure of Norbett's perfidy. Her right hand reached out and covered it and stilled it on her left wrist.

Norbett was saying, "When I went to high, I was always jealous of Johnny Malone because not only the teachers but the whole student body worshiped at his feet. And they all gave me a wide berth because I had a nasty disposition."

"Oh, come now," Johnny said uncomfortably.

But Norbett went on relentlessly, "And I always kept hoping that I'd find one person who would—sort of understand that I was ornery and smart aleck because— well, because I was covering up. I always wanted to find one person who would trust me—"

The hand squeezed Beany's heart harder. Oh, why had that wily Cynthia worked the seating arrangement so that she was next to Norbett, so that Miss Opal's comfortable bulk was between Beany and him? For suddenly she longed to reach out to him, to say softly, "Norbett, I trusted you until that night you didn't come to the band concert and then I saw you at the Ragged Robin with Cynthia."

Cynthia laughed. "The sooner you get over that corny idea of trusting people, and wanting somebody to trust you, the better off you'll be."

"No," Miss Opal said warmly. "Once you get over that —then you won't have much left. I've lived longer than any of you, and I've trusted everyone."

"Yes, and I'll bet you've had your leg pulled a lot, if you go through life thinking everyone is one of God's noblemen—or noblewomen."

"Yes, once in a while," Miss Opal confessed. "But, even so, I'd rather go on trusting and doing for the ones that are trustworthy. Go on, son," she said apologetically, "I shouldn't be talking when it isn't my turn."

"I was on the last paragraph anyway," Norbett ended lamely. "My goading ambition prompted my taking off for the coast. I thought I might get a big story out of it. I've always wanted to be a big newspaper man like Martie Malone. But maybe he's a big newspaper man because he's a big man."

"You're a big man in the making," Johnny said stanchly. "Don't be so humble, Uriah."

It was Miss Opal's turn next, but she nudged Beany and said, "You go ahead, Beany, the little fellow's just about asleep." She was patting him and crooning under her breath.

What could Beany say? She was all too conscious of Norbett, too resentful of Cynthia, sitting there so beautiful even in the lantern's meager light. And so derisive of candor and sincerity.

Johnny, like a genial master of ceremonies, said, "Beany Malone will be our next speaker. Beany needs no introduction. She is the helper of Eve Baxter, who helps the world. Eve says Beany is the best helper she ever had, owing to said Beany's heart's being as big as a prize Hubbard squash—and without the hard shell. If it weren't for Eve Baxter's holding her down, the Malone house would be given over to all the old derelicts and—"

Norbett said, "Are you telling Beany's story for her, or is she telling it? Go ahead, Beany. What are you going to California for?"

11

"—AND I'LL TELL YOU MINE"

Beany shifted her weight, covering her bare ankles with the faded-blue denim skirt. She said, "The morning Father told us good-by, he said that some people took trips in quest of something—and others to leave something behind. I guess I'm one of the runners-away. Even before Elizabeth's letter came, asking me to bring Martie to them in California, I wanted to go *some* place. I just felt I couldn't stand staying home—"

Norbett broke in, "You were happy as a lark that noontime, daubing paint on all the lawn furniture, and planning outdoor suppers even down to the last bean."

"I know," Beany said flatly, "and then—then—"

If only Cynthia weren't there! For she could feel the question in Norbett's thin face, feel his wanting to ask, "What happened, Beany?" But Cynthia *was* there, so she only ended thinly, "That's all. I just wanted to have a road

131

in front of me. Maybe—" she even tried a laugh but it came out frayed and ragged—"I wanted to send everyone I know post cards that said, 'Having a fine time. Wish you were here.' "

Even if she had wanted to say more, she wouldn't have had a chance because Cynthia said peremptorily, "Okay, Miss Opal, tell us why you're going to California." The very tense demand in her voice surprised Beany. Why would Cynthia *care* why Miss Opal was going?

Miss Opal took a long breath. "I'm going out with these folks because of a promise I made. In a way I hated to leave right now, just when my garden needed work on it every day but—"

"But why *are* you going then?" Cynthia insisted hurriedly.

"I guess I'd better go back twenty—no, twenty-two years ago," Miss Opal said unhurriedly. "I was nursing then—that was before my feet got to bothering me. I took a job of nursing a Mrs. Jason in Long Beach. Her husband was an oil man—a promoter, I guess you'd call it—and he was quite well-fixed then—"

"Then? What happened? Didn't he stay rich?" This time Norbett *did* nudge Cynthia to silence.

"Let her tell her story," Norbett said harshly.

Miss Opal's mind seemed looking back in the past. She went on, giving no heed to the interruption, "The poor soul was sick a long time with an obscure kind of anemia. And oh, a long, costly sickness it was. Mr. Jason was forever calling in specialists; one time he paid all expenses for a noted doctor to fly over from Vienna."

Cynthia stirred impatiently. Miss Opal continued,

"Poor Mr. Jason, what with her sickness and his losing money in bank failures, sort of turned bitter. Even then, I guess you'd call him eccentric and stubborn. I know when the government ordered everyone to turn in their gold pieces, he wouldn't do it. Well, I won't bore you with all that. Mrs. Jason died after being sick five years. That's when Mr. Jason broke up his home, and I came back to Colorado and bought the little acreage with my savings."

"Is that where you raised your boys?" Beany asked.

"I didn't raise them, lovey. I just helped out. One was a sickly little boy whose mother worked, and so I took him in and fed him up; and another had no home when his father deserted him—"

"What about Mr. Jason?" Cynthia prompted again.

"—and so I had him stay with me," Miss Opal finished her sentence, "until he was through high school. Mr. Jason moved around a lot after his wife died. But I always kept in touch with him. Every birthday I'd bake a hickory-nut cake with caramel icing and send it to him. He was always talking about coming back to Colorado. He had a niece here, and the niece had a baby, who was named Emily after Mr. Jason's wife. But I realized—though he never said so in words—that times were getting harder and harder for him, and he was more and more of a hermit. I've often thought of his wife's saying, 'Money that comes out of the ground doesn't last.' It's true. Money that you earn with your head or your hands stays with you longer than mining money or oil money."

"Did he ever come back to see his niece?" Johnny asked.

"He came back but he didn't get to see her," Miss Opal said regretfully. "It was a sad business all around. He came last Christmas. Of course, he was well along in years then—crowding eighty. He told me he had a feeling that his heart might go back on him, and he wanted to see them before he died. They lived in Laramie. So he went there by train and got off in that terrible blizzard around Christmas time. But his folks weren't home. They'd evidently gone off to spend the holidays with friends—that part of it, I don't know."

"Gosh, what did the poor old fellow do?" Johnny asked.

"He waited around for a bus and came down to Denver to see me. I've often wished he had telephoned me from the bus station. Somehow or other, I'd have got hold of a neighbor with a car to go get him. But instead he took the streetcar and then walked through the bitter wind and snow to find my little place. I'm quite a ways from the end of the line."

"And he died at your house, didn't he?" Cynthia put in.

Beany looked across at her, puzzled. How did Cynthia know so much about it? Or had Miss Opal mentioned before about old Mr. Jason's dying?

Again Miss Opal carried on her story, unheedingly: "My, it gave me a start when I opened the door that early morning. There he stood, so covered with snow I didn't know him. I couldn't get the poor man warm. He was shaking in a hard chill. He couldn't even hold the cup of hot coffee I hurried and made him. I saw he was a sick man. I'm a nurse myself but a bit rusty about all these new-fangled drugs. That's when I called in my nurse friend. Between us we took care of him for the ten days he lived—"

Norbett interrupted now, "What was the nurse's name?"

"Mary Rogers. Molly, we called her in nurse's training. And we did everything the doctor told us—but it was no use."

Norbett spoke again. "What doctor did you have?"

Miss Opal sat thoughtfully. "Let me see—"

Cynthia said belittlingly, "Maybe you've forgotten the doctor's name."

"Gilbraten," Miss Opal said, "Dr. Simon Gilbraten. I always have to stop and think of 'sauerbraten' before I can remember it. At that, I believe the poor man might have pulled through but for his heart. And he knew he wasn't going to make it. That's when he asked me to take care of the few things he had left. He'd been living on a little rented fruit farm near Oceanside. He had all his belongings in a heavy, horsehide trunk, and he said there was little of value in it—mostly old letters and keepsakes, and a few little gifts he had saved for folks who'd been nice to him during his lifetime. And so I gave him my promise and I'm only sorry I didn't go sooner."

"Why didn't you?" Cynthia, the interlocutor, wanted to know.

Again Miss Opal paused. "To tell the truth, the little money I could make on my chickens and eggs I had to pay this Dr.—" another pause while her mind fastened on 'sauerbraten'—"Gilbraten. He's been nice about his bill. He took chickens in part payment, and I kept his two dogs for him, too, when he and his family went on a trip."

Johnny said, "I'll bet Mr. Jason's niece and her little

girl felt bad that they missed seeing him. But I'll bet they were grateful to you for doing all you did for him."

"I never heard a word from them. The only one who came to see me and talk about Mr. Jason was a lawyer. My goodness, but he acted uppity. He even threatened me if I didn't turn over the key of the trunk to him. But I couldn't do that, after promising poor Mr. Jason that I'd carry out his wishes."

She turned to Cynthia to say with guileless faith, "You were saying something about this wide red-velvet belt I wear. Well, I'm absent-minded, and apt to mislay things, and I knew I'd be fidgety with worry about losing that key. So I sewed it inside this belt. I guess it is sort of a jarring color scheme but I feel safer when I'm wearing it."

Cynthia asked, "Is this place where the trunk is right in Oceanside?"

"No, it's about eleven miles out. That's another thing. Mr. Jason gave me the directions—he even had me draw a sketch, or a map, on a piece of paper. Once I lost the paper with it on, and that scared me so that I figured out a better way to keep it. Johnny, tilt your lantern over this way."

She took off her weathered black hat with the daisy trim and held it in the small arc of light from the ancient lantern. "I trimmed the directions right onto my hat. See this biggest blue daisy? That's Oceanside. And then I took this beige yarn that I happened to have and made six stitches, running northeast from it. This yellow daisy is the lemon orchard where he said you turned and kept going five or six miles. See, I made five stitches more. And this bunch of green leaves is the avocado ranch—or farm,

or whatever they call them. There's a small, one-room
tenant house there—and that's where the trunk is."

Beany squirmed uneasily. Though she couldn't say
why. She couldn't say why she wanted to nudge Miss Opal
and say, "You oughtn't to *tell* everybody."

Cynthia scrambled to her feet and said harshly, "Let's
get out of here. I'm anxious to see how Quaker's getting
along."

Little Martie was Beany's bedfellow that night. Beany
felt a wry sense of triumph at her maneuvering so that she
wouldn't be the one to sleep with Cynthia. She, Beany,
had sat on the edge of the double bed in which she had
deposited the sleeping child, while she undressed, thus
preëmpting it and leaving Miss Opal and Cynthia to share
the other one.

Beany wasn't sure whether Miss Opal was aware of the
stiff animosity between Beany and the new passenger or
not. Miss Opal, like Johnny, seemed to assume that all
God's children loved one another. H'mm!

Anyway, Miss Opal had remarked comfortably to
Cynthia while the girl untied the pink scarf from around
her head and shook loose her dark, abundant hair, "I
hope my snoring won't bother you, Cynthia. And if I take
up too much room, just shove me over."

All Cynthia said was, "I'm going to take a shower. I feel
all sticky from eating watermelon." She didn't ask her
other roommates if they wanted to take a shower, or if
they wanted to use the bathroom before she took over.
And she'll probably use all the hot water, Beany thought
glumly.

While the water splashed behind the closed door, Miss Opal planned aloud in housewifely fashion, "I believe we have enough rolls for breakfast, don't you, Beany? We can toast them in the oven. And we can use up the rest of the eggs that nice Burt gave us. Let's see, there'll be five grownups and the little fellow—"

"Five? There're only four of us and Martie."

"Norbett. Didn't you hear me ask him to drop over and have breakfast with us? No, I guess that was when you were carrying in the little fellow and putting him to bed."

"Did he say he'd come?" Beany's heart began a hard, excited pumping.

"He said he had to make some phone calls back to Denver in the morning. But he'll come—you'll see." She added with happy significance, "He wouldn't miss a chance of eating breakfast with you."

Beany couldn't go to sleep. She lay on, eyes closed but wide awake, long after Cynthia came out of the shower and leisurely put her hair up on curlers, and patted onto her face and neck and arms a cold cream with a heavy fragrance. Long after Cynthia turned out the light and crawled in beside her bulky partner. Long after Miss Opal's snores rose and fell rhythmically.

Once Beany sat up in bed to assemble the widely flung arms and legs of her small sleeping companion. In the dim light of the room she could see that Cynthia lay far over at the very edge on her side of the bed, and Beany couldn't help thinking, "I wish she'd fall out and raise a goose egg on her head."

Surely it was the strong coffee she had drunk at the picnic which kept her wearily awake, reliving the upsetting events of the day—Johnny's arriving and proudly presenting them with an added passenger (someone Beany's age who would be company for her!); Quaker's frightening green-tomato debauch; and, most jolting of all, Norbett Rhodes's appearing out of nowhere.

Suddenly Beany felt a restless and driven urge to *talk* to someone.

Cautiously she fumbled for her chintz housecoat hanging over the back of a chair. She pulled it about her and, in her bare feet, padded softly out of the room and into the night. She made her way to where Johnny lay like a dark cocoon on the leeward side of the building.

Johnny popped up in the bedroll—evidently he, too, had had trouble going to sleep. "Hi, little Beaver," he welcomed her in a whisper. "Sit down on one of these lumps of bedroll that isn't my legs."

Beany dropped down, snugging the skirt of the housecoat closer about her. In the dark background Quaker could be heard moving about, munching desultorily at the short, wiry grass. Well, thank heaven, Quaker had recovered from his indisposition because of Cynthia's ministering. Beany burst out almost without volition, "Cynthia's beautiful, isn't she?"

"Is she?" Johnny asked innocently. "I just felt she needed a hand, what with her axle's going out on her—and she was so shaky and tense when she told me she *couldn't* go back home, and that she *had* to get to California."

Oh, sure, sure, Beany thought. She put on a damsel-in-distress act, and you will always be a sucker for a damsel in distress.

Johnny was saying, "Gosh, Beany, do you realize how

lucky we Malones are? I did, when Cynthia was talking tonight out there at Fort Bridger. We've only got one parent but that's better than having four like Cynthia. When she talked about the fine art of chiseling—why, it sort of turned my stomach. And I've been lying here think-ing about—well, you remember my quoting from Great-Grandfather Malone's journal, that part about the ones who traveled 'well-found' helping the ones who weren't. In the old days it meant helping the other outfits by giving them axle grease, supplies, or cholera cures. But it came to me that it meant even more than that. What I mean is that that Cynthia gal hasn't got much—"

Beany wanted to say, "Hah! She's got two suitcases full of casual little originals with footwear to match. Not to mention all the creams, lotions, and perfumes." But Johnny's very seriousness stilled her bitter flippancy.

"She's got a sort of empty unhappiness inside." Strange, that eighteen-year-old Johnny should say almost the same thing as the older Miss Opal. "I keep thinking about you and Mary Fred and how you get more kick out of earning a buck than chiseling someone else out of five."

All this talk was fine, but Beany hadn't left her bed and come slipping out to sit hunched up on Johnny's bedroll to talk entirely about Cynthia. She veered the conversa-tion by saying, "I was—I mean, wasn't it a surprise to see Norbett?"

Johnny chuckled. "That Norbett! Coming all this way with some flimsy excuse about bringing you the dark glasses you left in his car. And muttering that he might possibly go on to California on a news story. I guess the poor guy didn't know what to do with himself with the Malones—especially Beany Malone—out of town."

Beany shifted unhappily, muttered, "I don't think that."

"Well, I do. And you know what I been thinking, Beany? I think Norbett's just hankering to go to California with us on his vacation. Just hanging around, waiting to be coaxed. It'd be fun if he went along, wouldn't it? We could sort of split up the load between the two cars. It'd be like a three-day picnic."

Again the very weight in Beany's heart pushed out her words, "Cynthia would be right there in the front seat of Norbett's car. Johnny, I think there's something between them."

"What d'you mean—something between them?"

Beany hesitated, all her feminine reluctance to bare her hurt and humiliation warring with the desire to share it, to ease it. Shakily, haltingly—at times hotly—she told Johnny about seeing Norbett and Cynthia together at the Ragged Robin after Norbett had told her he might be busy on a news story.

Even before she finished, Johnny reached out and shook her scoldingly as though she were the small Martie. "Beany, you little goop! What if they were? What does that prove? You heard Norbett say that he knew her father at the Park Gate Hotel. I'll bet Cynthia's father and step-mother had some other plans and so they foisted the gal off on Norbett."

Beany choked out, "Norbett doesn't foist off on easy. And if you could have seen him—bending across the table and looking so—so enthralled—"

"That's a nice word, pet. But I've seen Norbett look enthralled a lot of times with Beany Malone. You know, puddin'-head, you're good for Norbett. He's not all nettles and kinks—if I may mix metaphors—since he's known you. He needs someone who's warmhearted and under-standing and more or less forgiving like our Beaver."

You're so good, Johnny, she thought. You're like Miss Opal, seeing your own goodness in other folks. I'm not understanding or forgiving. When someone hurts me, I want to hurt him back.

Johnny added, "Don't you see, little one, that Norbett was pitching his whole talk to you tonight? I guessed he sensed that you were mad and hurt about *something*."

Again that strong hand squeezed Beany's heart. Then Johnny had noticed it, too. Johnny went on and his words were like healing ointment, "Why, honey, the poor guy was trying to say to you, 'Keep on trusting me, Beany, because I've got to have someone I can trust to trust me.' "

Beany's malice and rancor fairly sighed away with the night wind. She felt a rush of shame at her easy jumping to conclusions. Why had she been so stiff-necked? When Norbett met her on the boulevard and smiled warmly and said, "Do you think I'd let my girl walk home, loaded down like a pack mule?" why hadn't she said frankly, "I saw you last night at the Ragged Robin, and I've been brooding." Then Norbett would have filled in the why of his being there and all life would have been rosy again.

Johnny yawned widely and noisily. "Hey, we're on our way to California, remember? Vacation trip for Beany. Got to get rolling early in the morning. So skite back to bed because tough John Malone, wagon boss, will be routing you out at dawn."

Beany skited.

Their dark, crowded cottage camp seemed not sultry

and oppressive with the perfumed smell of Cynthia, but homey and friendly. The bed, gently warmed by the sleeping Martie received Beany. . . . Norbett was coming to breakfast in the morning. She would watch for him and go hurrying to meet him and say, "Norbett, you can trust me to keep on trusting you." No stubby Wyoming grass should grow under her feet until this enmity was smoothed out. She would mention seeing him with Cynthia. She could almost hear his scoffing rejoinder, "Well, ain't you the imaginative one!"

After all, a vacation wasn't a vacation when you carried a heavy lump inside you. Even though, in times of excitement, the lump lessened and disappeared, still there were so many things to remind her of Norbett—the tinkle of her bracelet for one thing.

She could stand Cynthia's arrogance, stand the worrying trailer full of roan horse, if only her heart was light. Oh, a vacation would be a real vacation if Norbett's red car traveled with theirs on the highway. If Beany rode in the seat beside him.

She was smiling when she fell asleep.

12

ROAD, BECKON HARDER!

The early morning bustle and hubbub! Of getting breakfast, of packing suitcases and cartons, of dressing Martie. Beany's heart had its own hubbub. She dressed her small nephew, hoping that Miss Opal, or at least Cynthia, wouldn't notice how her eyes kept glancing out the square window, how many times she walked to the open door and glanced out. She said, "Stand still, wiggleworm, if you want me to fasten this holster belt on you."

"And don't be shooting that silly cap pistol all the time," Cynthia said impatiently. "If you have to, go outdoors."

Miss Opal, the peacemaker, offered, "Why don't you leave your caps here, sonny, and you run down and see how Quaker is this morning?"

"But don't go near him. And don't you give him a thing to eat," Cynthia snapped. "I'll take care of Quaker." Her tone implied, "I'm the only one capable of taking care of a horse." She went out the door with a fine disregard about who was to carry out and load her two matched suitcases in the car.

Miss Opal bustled about with breakfast preparations. She was toasting rolls in the doll-sized oven. "This is the last of the rolls. But we've a loaf of bread left. I'll wrap it and we can pick up some lunch meat for sandwiches at noon. We still have two cans of fruit and a glass of strawberry jam and one of chokecherry."

"I don't know what we'd have done without all that food you brought along," Beany said gratefully. She fastened the catch on her suitcase, gathered up a little red wad that was one of Martie's socks, put it with its mate, and fastened Martie's grip. She would carry these out; she could keep a better lookout for Norbett if she was outside.

Miss Opal said, "There, the rolls are buttered and ready. Where did you say Johnny went?"

"He went out to see about getting a spare tube. He's a little worried about that left rear tire."

Miss Opal was just adding, "Maybe he'll run into Norbett and bring him back with him," when Martie came hurrying in and imparted, "Norbett's here already. He's out there with Cynthia."

"He is!" Beany ejaculated.

"Yeh, he's helping her feed Quaker. I wanted to help but Norbett told me to come on back."

The grips Beany picked up felt suddenly heavier than they had before. She carried them outside. She couldn't keep her eyes from turning toward the end of the row of cottage camps. Yes, there was Norbett. Cynthia was standing at the head of the roan horse, running her fingers through his mane while Quaker breakfasted.

Norbett stood close to her. Norbett must have been watching for Cynthia, waiting to get her away from the rest of them. He must have something very private to say to her when he didn't want even a small boy within hearing distance.

Beany carried the bags to the car. Some of the luggage must be crowded into the back seat, she thought drearily. She lifted them in and tried to concentrate on how best to arrange them. She picked up her jacket to refold it, and the bobby pins in the pocket showered to the floor. Maybe she would need them—though what did it matter whether she ever put her topknot of hair up in curls or not? She dropped to her knees on the floor of the car to pick up the shiny slivers of metal.

She was both glad—and sorry—that she was out of sight, for Norbett and Cynthia came around the car to the corner of their cottage court and stopped. But Beany was not out of hearing. Through the open car windows she heard Norbett say, "Cynthia, please change your mind and go back. I can take you back with me."

Cynthia answered, "Oh, stop all the winning sales talk. Once I make up my mind, it stays made up. I told you I was going to California, and I'm going."

"I can't let you go alone. If you go, I'll go along with you."

"You'll do nothing of the kind, Norbett."

"All right then—but I'm fed up on all this secrecy. I know I promised——"

Cynthia gave a short, mocking laugh. "Yes, I know, I know. As any fool can plainly see, Beany is carrying the torch for you—and so you——"

At that very moment Beany's suitcase, which she had hurriedly set on the back seat until she could gather up the bobby pins, slid to the floor. It bashed Beany on her knee and knocked open the car door, which hadn't been shut tight, and fell out of the car. Beany, looking up from where she was crouched on the floor, saw on both Norbett's and Cynthia's face startled surprise.

With all the dignity she could muster, she unfolded herself and stepped out. She said, "Do you mind if I correct you, Cynthia? I don't happen to be carrying a torch for Norbett. That's why I'm going to California—because I got so sick of seeing him around. Oh, and Norbett—this bracelet. I was so busy getting ready I—I forgot to take it off."

Cynthia gave an airy laugh, said, "Excuse me, this looks like a private fight," and turned and walked on into their cottage camp.

Some of the bobby pins slithered to the ground as Beany's fumbling fingers worked at the bracelet clasp. Finally it came undone and Beany thrust the clinking weight of silver at Norbett. "Here! Maybe you know someone else you'd like to wear your charm bracelet."

She braced herself for his angry retort—maybe his, "Well, thanks, maybe I do." But he only looked at her with a queer tight look on his face and backed away from her outstretched hand. His very lack of anger made her more furious. She flung the bracelet at him. It thudded against his chest under the green sport shirt.

Why didn't he say something—anything? Why didn't he pick up the bracelet instead of letting it lie in the trampled grass?

And oh, why couldn't they have a private fight? But no, here came Miss Opal hurrying out the door, her face flushed from breakfast-getting. And here came Johnny, carrying a packaged inner tube and saying without preamble, "Hey, Norb, how about joining our California trek? Beany and I were talking about it last night and what a lark it would be."

Beany walked over to her fallen suitcase. She heard Norbett's flustered, "No—that is, I don't know. I put in some phone calls to Denver early this morning. To a fellow who works with me on the *Tribune*. It—well, it sort of depends on what he says—whether I'll go—or not."

Beany carried the suitcase to the car while Miss Opal pressed hospitably, "Come on in and have breakfast with us, Norbett. It's all ready."

Beany wouldn't look up or join in the conversation. She heard Norbett answer, "I don't believe I'd better—I have to wait for this phone call to come in."

A small, waiting silence. Well, they needn't look to her to coax him. She felt Norbett's eyes turning to her, and her face set more grimly. And then, even though Johnny was saying, "Well, heck, we can wait till your call comes through," and Miss Opal was insisting, "The coffee's ready to be poured—and you look like you need a cup," Norbett turned, and with a forced, "Hope you have a nice trip," strode off.

When breakfast was over Beany passed the spot where Norbett had stood when she banged the bracelet at him. No shiny bit of silver lay in the trampled grass. Not that Beany Malone would have stooped over and picked it up, if it had! Not that Beany Malone cared what happened to it!

Thus began the fourth day of Beany's vacation trip.

They crossed the Utah state line at ten o'clock that morning. With Quaker staring contentedly over the top of his trailer; with the wired-on bale of alfalfa only half a bale now. With Cynthia riding comfortably in the front seat beside Johnny. With Martie regretting that all his caps were used up. (Though he was the only one who regretted it.) With Miss Opal musing, "Mattie said she'd keep the bucket of tomato bush until we came through. There are a few little tomatoes that the poor innocent missed, and they may make tomatoes yet."

With Beany holding a stiff cloak of anger about her. Anger was numbing. And preferable to the weight of hurt that stabbed under the ribs.

Utah, the long state! There was no cutting across half of it as they had Colorado, no sidling across a corner of it as they had Wyoming. Almost its whole length must be traversed. On the map which rattled on Beany's lap, Highway 91 stretched like a narrow red ribbon—a ribbon which had been tied in tight knots and then halfway smoothed out. A ribbon with little polka dots which were towns with names. They slowed and passed through them, and the names became blurred to indistinctness in their minds—Castle Rock, Echo City—

It was when they were leaving Echo City, after stopping at a filling station, that Johnny handed Beany the billfold. "Beany, I hereby make you the Keeper of the Exchequer. Maybe," he said ruefully, "you can hang onto a dollar tighter than I can."

Beany counted it. "Johnny, isn't there more than this— more than thirty-eight dollars and twenty-three cents left?"

"Is that all? Gosh, and we had seventy to start with after we paid for the battery."

Beany thought aloud, "I spent about ten dollars for the thermos jug and Martie's haircut and his Levis and the dog meat—and dark glasses . . ." Norbett had brought the glasses back. Don't think about Norbett, she warned herself. Think about finances.

Mattie had charged them ten dollars for their two nights at the cottage court. She usually charged ten a night, she explained, for the ones with two double beds, bath, and kitchenette during tourist season; but because of Miss Opal's friendliness and helpfulness she cut it in half for them. Gas and oil, the adjusting of the brake which grabbed too tight, the new inner tube, the oats for Quaker. *And* the dollar fifty for the watermelon which Cynthia had seen and desired.

Down Utah's smooth highway Johnny drove while Beany sat in the back seat, her mind a hodgepodge of mental arithmetic and mental anguish.

She added the miles they had put behind them. One hundred and twenty-five to Laramie, plus 117 to Medicine Bow, plus 109 to their stopping place near Fort Bridger. They had gone about 440 miles of the 1268— Oh, but wasn't she thankful she hadn't, this early morning in her mistaken regret, gone rushing to Norbett to say, "You can trust me to keep on trusting you." Wouldn't that have been a laugh, when Norbett's only thought was to see Cynthia and beg her to go back with him? . . .

They had covered only about a third of the way to California. And of the ninety dollars Elizabeth had sent for the trip, they had thirty-eight dollars and twenty-three cents left. It didn't make sense. Yet they had needed to buy every-thing they had bought. All, except the watermelon! Beany looked at the back of Cynthia's dark hair rippling over the pale pink sweater which topped her palm beach skirt. The jacket of the suit was carefully folded over the back of the front seat. Again and again Miss Opal restrained the fidgety Martie from mussing it. You won't catch me spending any dollar and a half for a watermelon for you, Beany vowed spleenishly.

. . . "Cynthia, please don't go to California," Norbett had besought. He hadn't said anything like that to Beany Malone when she told him she was going. He hadn't said, "Then I'll go with you. . . ."

If it took them three days and fifty-one dollars and seventy-seven cents to go a third of the way, how long would it take and how much would it cost to go the remaining two thirds? Well, it jolly well better not take them six more days, and it jolly well *couldn't* cost them two times fifty-one dollars and seventy-seven cents because they had only thirty-eight dollars and twenty-three cents.

"Johnny, we've got about 830 miles yet to go. How much gas will that take?"

Johnny concentrated while he fell in behind a huge truck. "About fifty gallons. Even if we pay thirty cents a gallon, that'll only be fifteen dollars. We're not burning much oil. We oughtn't to have to buy any more rations for Quaker. Don't worry, little Beaver. One more night on the road, and then we'll pull in to Oceanside and our troubles will be over."

They stopped on the main street of a town to buy lunch meat. Beany said, "I'll buy it." She didn't dare let

Johnny stand in front of a meat counter. Johnny couldn't buy a small amount of anything. Beany would buy twenty-three cents' worth, no more, no less.

She came back to the car to find Cynthia there alone. Johnny had gone to fill their thermos jug with fresh water. And Martie had set up such a wail for cookies with pink icing that Miss Opal had diverted his mind by taking him across the street to show him some squealing pigs in a truck.

Cynthia added, "I knew it would be like this. Kids are *always* wanting something. If they can't think of anything else they want to stop to go to a rest room." She was rubbing at a spot on her jacket with her handkerchief; Martie must have put it there once when Miss Opal's watchful eye relaxed. "And they're always pawing over everything with sticky hands."

Something clicked in Beany's mind. A petulant, arrogant voice which had said almost those same words to Beany over the telephone. Beany said, "Cynthia, you telephoned to our house, didn't you, and asked to go to California with us? You wanted us to take you and send Martie on the train?"

For a brief moment she thought Cynthia was going to deny it. But she only said with a shrug of defiance, "So what? I still think it would have been a good idea."

Beany said slowly, "And that day I said to you, 'Why don't you drive out by yourself if you're so particular?' and you said, 'I would if I had a car.'"

"So what?"

"You told Johnny that you were driving out to California and that—well, somehow you ran off the road and broke an axle. You lied. You don't have a car at all."

Again for a brief moment Beany thought she had the unwelcome guest cornered. But only for a brief moment. Cynthia challenged, "I suppose you never told a thing in in your life that wasn't the whole truth, and nothing but the truth? I suppose you can't wait to run and tell Johnny how I lied. You're the type. You can't wait to turn Johnny against me and have him hate me because you do."

Beany found herself saying stiffly, "No, I'm not going to run and tell Johnny." She couldn't say why she said it, why she had no desire to. Was it because her enmity for Cynthia was so mixed with her hurt pride, her quarrel with Norbett? She only added, "I still don't see why you wanted to go with *us*."

"Maybe because the bus drivers wouldn't take me out there on faith, and you nice Malones would. Maybe because I liked your company."

We're stuck with her, Beany thought despairingly, as she looked up and saw Johnny returning with the thermos of water, as Miss Opal and Martie returned, and Miss Opal said, "We can open a jar of peaches for dessert. We've enough paper cups to eat them out of."

And Cynthia turned on her charm for Johnny, her "wonderful, loveable you" manner. She laughed throatily at every remark he made. She teased him about having hollow legs when, after gulping down his sandwich, he finished the loaf of Miss Opal's bread, using mustard for sandwich filling. She said as she flicked crumbs off her lap, "Oh, Johnny, you're priceless. This is so much more fun than going on a bus. It was sweet of you to make room for me."

Beany did her stint of driving that afternoon. Johnny said, "Let's do a little shifting. We'll take Big Ears up here with Beany and me. And, Cynthia, you and Miss Opal can take it easy in the back seat with only a jar or two of peaches to roll on your heads."

Beany's spirits lifted as she drove. Her dark glasses broke the sun's white glare. The road beckoned, the road lulled. If they kept on making such good time their thirty-eight dollars would nicely see them to Oceanside. There wasn't much traffic, so if the trailer rocked a little, let Quaker rock with it.

No bracelet clinked on her arm to remind the California-bound Beany of that other naïve little Barberry Street Beany. . . . Norbett *must* have picked up the bracelet. . . . Look at how swiftly and painlessly Kay forgot Johnny once she left Denver.

Miles, mountains, small towns fell behind them—Mona, Nephi, Levan. And always the highway sign "91" giving them the friendly nod which assured them, "You're on the right road." She felt a little superior to the stay-at-homes they passed, who were following the mundane routine of pushing lawn mowers or returning from market with food for the next meal. Beany Malone was on the wing. She even felt a certain kinship with Mary Fred's dentist, who could clip out the distance in two days.

A longer stretch between Levan and the next town. Beany's bare arm that rested on the window ledge turned pinker and pinker in the sun. Johnny dozed beside her. Truck drivers were helpful, friendly. One, in an oil truck in front of her, motioned her to pass him. She did it neatly.

waved her thanks, and he grinned and tooted his horn. Miss Opal paid tribute, "My, Beany, you're a wonderful driver."

Beany sang as she drove. She'd show Cynthia how heartbroken and crushed she was!

Johnny stirred, yawned. "Better stop at the next town for gas, Lily Pons."

The sun was dropping lower. Beany said, "How'd it be if we stopped and picked up something to eat and drove on for maybe another hundred miles? I'm not tired."

They drew into a filling station. Beany was just pocketing the change when the truck driver she had passed drove in. He stopped to scratch Quaker's nose as he walked by. He backed off then and looked at their license plate. "I thought when you passed me you had a Colorado license. And that's a Dodge you're driving. Did the road patrol catch up with you?"

They looked at him amazedly. "Road police, you mean?" Johnny asked. "No. What for?"

"One of the stops I made—let's see, was it before I hit Provo or afterwards? Anyway, it was about midmorning when I stopped to deliver some oil, and I heard a road patrolman asking the fellow at the station if he'd seen a Dodge with a Colorado license plate. He said there'd be either a young fellow or girl driving it."

Cynthia's hand, which had been uplifted to push back her hair, dropped limply. "What else did he say—the road patrolman that was looking for the car? Was it someone in the car he wanted stopped?"

"Blamed if I know what the deal was. As I say, I was

delivering oil and I just happened to hear them asking the fellow at the station if he'd seen anything of a Dodge '41, dragging a horse trailer."

"But I can't imagine why they'd want to stop us. My sister and I both have driver's licenses," Johnny said worriedly.

The truck driver studied them. His eyes rested on Miss Opal's pink, honest face, on the little boy clinging to her skirts. He gave a stick of gum to him and wadded two between his own lips. He asked, half jokingly, "You haven't got any stolen property along with you, have you? I remember once my brother-in-law was moving to Kansas and, by heck, just because he hadn't paid for the electric icebox he was taking along, they stopped his truck and took it away from him. There's a law that you can't take unpaid-for goods across the state line. That horse belongs to you, doesn't he?"

"Quaker? Well, not exactly," Johnny said. "We're taking him out to a friend of ours. But he'll be paid for just as soon as we get there."

"You don't have a bill of sale for him, huh?"

"No—we don't. You see, it was like this," and Johnny proceeded to outline the story of Quaker, the lost roping horse; of Mary Fred running the ad; of Ander, who was waiting for him with open arms and open checkbook at Oceanside.

Beany added honestly, "The farmer that owned him told us not to take him away. But we had to. We couldn't leave him there alone. We just intended to take him to Wyoming to Ander. Golly, this is Tuesday—and the man said he'd come in on Monday."

The truck driver chewed his gum thoughtfully. "Now that just might be it. You don't know of anyone else that'd want to stop you, do you?"

Everyone said no. Everyone except Cynthia, who said nothing.

"Tell you what I'd do if I was you kids," he advised. "I'd get off Highway 91. Might just be this old fellow you bought the horse from—or almost did—is kicking up a rumpus. But, cripes, if your friend that owned the horse is out there waiting— You got a map?"

Beany produced the already rumpled map and, with a stubby finger, the driver pointed out, "See this little road cutting off here? It's a dirt road but it'll get you over to 89. About twenty-five, twenty-seven miles. Chances are they won't be figuring on you taking 89. It's not a bad road either—used to drive it myself. Yessir, you keep off this main drag tomorrow and I'll bet you can get through all right."

"Let's go on then," Cynthia said sharply.

13

THE RED BELT

This was a new experience, this feeling that the road police were looking for them, were ready to clamp a heavy hand upon them, or perhaps the trailer containing Ander's roping horse. Their only thought was flight, to get off the main highway as speedily as possible. When an affable young filling station attendant sauntered up to wipe off their windshield, Johnny motioned him away.

"Never mind. We're in a hurry."

This time Cynthia didn't maneuver herself in the front seat beside Johnny. She was the first one in the back seat. She even held the door open and reached out a helping hand to the slower-moving Martie and Miss Opal. "Hurry —hurry!"

Johnny took the wheel, muttering as he swung out of the station, "We'll pick up something to eat. There ought to be some place on that little road that cuts across the mountains to 89."

They breathed easier once they turned off on the road that led out of town and toward the southeast. Beany had to bend over close to study the map for it was growing dark. On it the road was marked blue, like a striped piece of blue hose. On the map it stretched, with only a southeast slant, from the red ribbon that was 91 to a slimmer red ribbon that was 89.

But the road they took wound in and out of mountains, across narrow bridges. Dark storm clouds pushed in front of the setting sun. Thunder rumbled, and lightning zig-zagged until Miss Opal muttered often and fervently, "Bless us and save us!"

They climbed mountains so steep that the weight of the trailer caused them to shift—to shift again, and to labor slowly to the top. They descended mountains on hairpin curves with the weight of the trailer shoving them forward. Windshield wipers clicked against the lashing rain. They met a detour sign that sent them skirting wide off a stretch of road under construction. The rain poured, and the car and trailer sloshed and skidded.

Afterwards they were never sure how they lost their way —whether the rain obscured the sign that would have directed them back to the road or whether the sign had been blown down. But they kept on and on, feeling their way along, shivering with chill before they groped for sweaters, sitting on the edge of their seats and trying to joke about it. "Be funny if we found ourselves back in Denver."

Johnny's wavy black hair was like wet feathers; Beany's medium brown clung damply to her head, for they constantly had to let down car windows to try to get their bearings. Martie took this time to whimper dismally about his tooth's hurting, his foot's hurting—when, of course, it was only that he was hungry, chilled, and frightened, along with the rest of them.

Finally Johnny stopped the car. He tried to make his voice casual. "Just as soon as this downpour lets up a little, I'll take the flashlight and go exploring. You'd think there'd be some sign of human habitation around here."

"I'll go with you," Beany said.

There seemed little chance of the rain's letting up, so after what seemed a long wait—though it was only ten minutes—Johnny and Beany got out. They were on a rutted mountain road, and they tramped on ahead until, looking back, the car lights were only pale and small yellow blurs.

Then suddenly the flashlight's ray of light caught the bars of a wooden gate. They opened it and went through in shaky trepidation, feeling like unwelcome trespassers. "There's a house—or a sort of cabin," Johnny muttered. "Don't go flashing your light around, or whoever is inside might get wrathy and set their dogs on us. Should we call or knock?"

Beany knocked timidly. No one answered it. Johnny knocked louder. Beany said between his knocks, which became more insistent, "I imagine it's a week-end cabin like we have in our Colorado mountains. Oh, Johnny—" as a drenching gust of rain soaked them—"don't you suppose it'd be all right to go in? We'd leave everything just the way we found it."

"It's locked," Johnny said, trying the door. "I'd hate to break in a place but, gee, I hate to think of little Martie and Miss Opal and all of us having to wait in the car till morning to find our way."

Beany flashed the light around. She had been to mountain cabins often with friends. And usually the key was left in some safe niche. She looked under the soaked rubber door-mat. She felt on the ledge above the door. She saw a flat stone lying near the step. She turned it over and there, with a blue cord showing in the flashlight, was a key. And it fitted.

Their hearts pounding, they entered. The flashlight disclosed a small, tidy kitchen, a big living room beyond with a fireplace in it. They trod lightly, spoke in whispers like fugitives. "There's a bedroom opening off the living room. Look, Johnny, there's wood in the fireplace all ready to light. Wouldn't a fire feel good?"

They sloshed back to the car. Slowly, carefully they made the climb up the road and through the gate. It was hard to follow the dim ruts and once the trailer gave a twisting lurch which jerked the car sideways. Johnny got out, came back to report cheerfully, "The trailer's still got both wheels and Quaker is still in one piece. We hit a gnarled tree stump."

They cleaned their muddy feet before entering. Beany gave a nervous giggle. "I feel like Goldilocks going into the three bears' house while they were out." They lighted the wood in the fireplace; and Miss Opal scolded Beany and Cynthia into changing to dry clothes, for Cynthia had unloaded Quaker, fitted him nicely into the woodshed, and fed him. "He won't need water, will he?" Johnny asked. "Can't he just lick himself off?"

In their own hungry desperation they looked through

cupboards. "A box of soap powder which might be nice made into an omelet," Johnny said. "A jar of olives, pancake flour, and a can of asparagus. Oh, and a little chunk of cheese in a jar."

They made a fire in the kitchen range and Miss Opal stirred up pancakes, which they spread with her choke-cherry jelly. They found coffee and drank it black. They ate hungrily, yet uneasily, each one fearful of every sound. Fearful that the owners of the cabin should return and find them.

Unlike Goldilocks, none of them slept soundly that night. None, unless it was little Martie, and even he insisted on having his gun and holster handy.

They didn't undress. They only eased belts that were tight, slipped off their wet shoes, and arranged them in front of the fire to dry. Miss Opal and Martie lay on the big bed in the curtained-off bedroom. Cynthia and Beany each lay on one side of the fireplace on the short window seats. Johnny sat in a rocker, his long legs stretched out to a straight chair. The owners of the cabin might be city folks who would come up late after work. The intruders felt, somehow, that they would seem less the intruders if they were caught fully dressed. At every sound they stiffened to guilty alertness.

Beany wakened in the early morning, cramped, chill, and unrested. It was Johnny's rattling at the kitchen stove which brought her dazedly to her feet. She slid her feet into huaraches that had dried to tight stiffness. Johnny said in a whisper—no one had raised his voice after crossing the threshold— "It's getting daylight. I'll stir up some pancakes, so we can be on our way."

Goaded by an uneasy feeling of urgency, they hurried their departing preparations. Only Martie seemed unhampered by their disquieting dread. He played about, draping a black bearskin rug over him until Cynthia, when Johnny was out of earshot, commanded sharply, "Stop doing that! You almost tripped me."

Johnny mixed the breakfast pancakes while Miss Opal, with Beany's help, put the rooms in the same neat order in which they had found them. Cynthia watered Quaker, fed him the last of the oats. A tense, scurrying daybreak.

Johnny, with his usual inability to mix up a small amount of anything, baked more pancakes than they could eat. "All to the good," he said, putting them in a paper bag. "Come noon we'll be ravenous."

After his night of uneasy vigilance, Johnny's black eyes looked big and heavy in his thin face. Yet it was Johnny's exuberance which put heart in them all. "This noon we'll stop in some sequestered spot—and wait till you see what I turn out for you in a skillet! One of these memorable events you'll be telling your grandchildren about."

Cynthia said, "Oh, Johnny, you're wonderful. I never knew anyone like you." She said it impulsively, sincerely. This time, Beany realized, it wasn't a line.

Johnny and Beany chopped wood to replace the fuel they had used. They left a note on the kitchen table.

We had to use your cabin last night because we got lost in the rain. If you ever come to Denver, call on the Malones on Barberry Street and we'll return your hospitality.

Miss Opal weighted it down with her remaining jar of peaches as a gift offering. Beany looked through her suitcase and found a bar of scented soap which her chum, Kay, had given her for Christmas. She left it beside the jar of fruit. "I always thought," she whispered to Miss Opal, "that Goldilocks was an ungrateful little wench to run out of the bears' house without ever a thank you."

They replaced the key under the flat rock.

A hot sun sucked up mist from the mountain world as they set out. The trailer rocked dangerously on its two wheels as they felt their way down the rutted road and found the detour which had detoured them too widely the night before. A few hours' driving brought them to Highway 89.

At first they drove in trepidation, mindful of every car that came toward them, that passed them. But no road patrolman stopped them. Again the miles, the towns fell behind Beany as she drove and Johnny in the back seat, with a blanket lumped under his head, slept. They were hungry long before noon because of their early and hasty breakfast. Johnny roused, said, "I should like to stop at the next town, driver."

Beany commented happily, "We've already made over a hundred miles and it isn't eleven yet."

The town they stopped at was Panguitch. "Only a dollar bill, I pray thee," Johnny said, extending his hand. "Don't give me any more because in my ravenous state I could buy out the store."

Beany extracted the dollar bill. Their funds, what with two stops for gas and oil, and minus this dollar, added up to thirty dollars and seventeen cents.

They drove another twenty miles of up and down mountains before they found a place to stop. They pulled off the main road and took one that led to a mountain clearing. Johnny started a fire of pine twigs. Cynthia let Quaker out of the trailer and walked him about to limber him. Gratefully he sniffed the small tufts of grass, nibbled at a few wild flowers.

Beany took this opportunity to mend the ripped pocket of the cowboy shirt Martie wore. "You can take the shirt-tail out," Martie condescended, "but I don't want to take the shirt clear off."

Miss Opal said as she handed her needle and thread, "I'd do it, Beany, but I want to sort through everything in my big cretonne bag."

As Beany sewed, she watched Johnny's activities around Martie's small figure. Johnny unwrapped a lump of sausage and put it in the skillet, chopping it apart with the same penknife he used to open cans. When the sausage was brown and sputtery, he dumped in two cans of spaghetti, a can of corn, a small tin of ripe olives. She saw him rummage hopefully through the car to see if there was something else he might add.

Beany bent over the little boy to bite off her thread; she tucked the shirt in carefully, said fondly, "Goodness, Martie, you'll have to build up some hips to hold up that holster."

Johnny called, "Bring out the crepes suzette, Beany. Gather round, folks, with your eatable plates."

Each one held out a pancake and Johnny heaped it high with the hot mixture. Each one ate it, holding a hand under it so that if a morsel spilled over it would not be lost.

Beany ate hers hungrily, yet puzzledly. There it was again, that same unusual and baffling flavor she had noticed the noontime Johnny served them his Jim Bridger stew—his I-haven't-the-slightest-idea stew. She recognized that same nutlike taste and fragrance.

She finished it thoughtfully, asked, "Johnny, what was it you found in the car at the very last, and dumped in the skillet with the other stuff?"

"Never mind," Johnny said largely. "It was something in a can that looked and smelled edible. Kind fate must have put it in the car for just this occasion."

Beany's curiosity was too much for her. She walked over to where Johnny had tossed the cans. She stood for an amazed moment, staring down at the round blue can with its pried-off lid which kept company with the two empty spaghetti cans, the one with a pictured ear of corn on it, the smaller tin in which olives had come.

She stooped and picked up the blue one, smelled of it, and waved it accusingly, "John Esmond Malone, do you know what you did? You dumped in my almond meal— what was left in the can. Kind fate didn't put it there. Mary Fred did."

"Okay, Catherine Cecilia Malone, then we can thank Mary Fred."

"But it was to take freckles off," Beany said. "You're not supposed to eat it. Kay's mother told me to make a paste and coat over the freckles."

"Hah!" Johnny said. "I'd say it went for a better purpose than removing freckles, if you know what I mean."

Beany ignored that thrust. "I wondered what happened to that can with some in it that I kept in our cupboard. You put it in your Jim Bridger stew that day—"

"And it was a culinary success, if I do say so," Johnny

defended. "No one died from it. I even heard such adjectives as 'indefinable, illusive.' Why shouldn't one deviate from the norm?"

Cynthia laughed heartily. "Oh, Johnny, you said it would be a memorable event. But I'm going to lock up my lemon lotion before you use it for pie filling."

"I never tasted anything better," Miss Opal paid tribute. "And, Beany, buttermilk is just as good for freckles."

"Nothing is any good for freckles," Beany admitted, and joined in the laughter. She started to say, "Just wait till I tell—" but she stopped short, and her laughter stopped or rather changed to something near to tears. She had meant to say, "Just wait till I tell Norbett," before she remembered that she would never be telling Norbett anything again.

Strange, how a sudden ache of memory could slip up on her unaware. It wasn't fair—it wasn't fair! When you vowed to yourself, "I'm going to forget," you ought to be able to forget. She walked away from the hilarious little group and dropped down. If tears must fall, she wouldn't let Cynthia see.

Johnny called after her, "Now you know the secret ingredient, Beany. Now what are you going to think about when you wake up in the night?"

Plenty, Beany thought wretchedly, plenty.

In the lacework of sun and shade Martie collected pine cones. Johnny sat relaxed. Cynthia came over and sat beside him, lifting her dark hair in the cooling breeze. Beany pretended to be absorbed in the view.

Only Miss Opal moved about nervously. Again she sat on the car's running board and emptied in her lap the contents of the capacious cretonne bag Johnny called the Mother's Helper. She sorted carefully through all the odds and ends. She climbed into the car and picked up each blanket, cushion, and sweater and shook it out, refolded it. Finally she asked, "Johnny, would it be too much trouble for you to open the luggage compartment and take out my suitcase so I can look through it?"

Beany got to her feet. "What are you looking for, Miss Opal?"

"Oh, if I weren't so addlepated," came the harried answer. "You know I never take it off, but last night, somehow, it felt so tight and binding, and I was so tired that I unfastened it and hung it over the back of a chair near the bed. And then this morning—well, you know how hurried we were—and I can't remember. I thought maybe I might have put it in my suitcase without thinking."

"Your red belt, you mean?" Beany asked. "With the key sewed in it? Oh, my goodness, wouldn't it be awful if you left it back at that cabin where we stayed? Did anybody see the red belt?"

Johnny only shook his head soberly. Cynthia showed no interest whatever.

Martie looked up from where he sat on the ground, piling pine cones together. "Cynthia's got it," he said. "She took it."

14

EXIT CYNTHIA

Miss Opal was the first to speak following Martie's startling announcement. She reproached him gently. "You shouldn't say things like that, honey."

He said positively, "But she did. I saw her take it. I was rolled up in the black fur rug, and I knew she'd be mad at me if she saw me so I laid real still and peeked out. It was on the chair, and she took it and rolled it up like this—" he made a rolling motion with his dusty hands—"and then she put it in her pocketbook. I'll show you."

He leaped to his feet, started toward the large boulder beside which Cynthia's scarf and woven pouch bag lay. Cynthia took swift, intercepting steps. She snapped out angrily, "Don't you touch my bag."

For perhaps ten seconds no one spoke. Martie crept back to Beany, half whimpering, "I was peeking out from under that black fur rug—and I kept real still—so she wouldn't be mad at me."

Miss Opal was breathing hard; her face looked anxious

and drained, but she managed to say, "Oh, I'm glad you did pick it up, child, for I might have gone off and left it. I'll put it back on and after this I'll be more careful."

Cynthia didn't answer. She stood clutching the bag to her defiantly. Johnny turned and confronted her. "Give her the belt with the key in it, Cynthia."

"I won't," Cynthia said, tossing back her dark mane of hair. "I'll give her the belt, but I won't give her the key."

"Oh yes, you will," Johnny said evenly. "You haven't any right to keep it."

"She's the one who hasn't any right to it," Cynthia hurled back. "Just because she pulled the wool over old Uncle Jason's eyes, and over the eyes of you Malones with all her nicey-nice talk, is no sign she can fool me."

"*Your* Uncle Jason?" Beany put in.

"Yes, my *Great*-Uncle Jason. And I'm his heir. My mother was his niece and the only relative he has living. That makes Mother and me inherit everything he's got."

Miss Opal said weakly, "But, Cynthia, he hasn't got anything. He was a poor man when he died."

"That's what you say."

"Wait a minute," Johnny said. "*Cynthia!* That wasn't the name of the baby Mr. Jason's niece had. She named it after Mr. Jason's wife, didn't she, Miss Opal?"

"Emily. That was his wife's name. And I remember Mr. Jason writing me and telling me that his niece had named her baby, Emily—"

"She did," Cynthia said. "Emily Cynthia. By the time I was in junior high, I hated the name, so I took Cynthia. Emily! It sounds like something out of *David Copperfield*." She turned to Johnny, as though she were sure she could win him to her side. "Listen, Johnny. From the time I can remember, my mother always talked about her rich Uncle Jason. And you heard Miss Opal say that night at Fort Bridger—she probably didn't mean to say it, but it slipped out—that he was always a rugged individual, who wouldn't let anyone boss him around. And that when the government called in all the gold he refused to turn his in. Mother said that when she went out to see him—that was before I was born—he had sacks and sacks of gold pieces. He put through big business deals with gold because he had lost money in banks when they failed, and he never trusted them. Mother said he had a lot of mesh bags so filled with gold pieces you could hardly lift them."

"So what?" Johnny said. "That was before you were born. Do you suppose the old man would be living in a one-room shack on somebody's rented farm, and be so poor he had to take a streetcar instead of a taxi that blizzardy morning he went to Miss Opal's, if he had gold pieces stashed away?"

"I certainly do! I think he came to see my mother and me to tell us that he had it and to leave us the key. But it so happened that we weren't home, and he went down to see Miss Opal. He was old and sick, and she got around him. Either that, or else he left her the key to give to us. But, of course, she'd never admit that. That's why she's so ginned up to get out there. You aren't fool enough, are you, to think she'd trek clear across almost thirteen hundred miles, when her feet swell up every night, if she thought there were just a few little folderol keepsakes in that trunk for her to distribute to dear old friends? Fooie!"

"Yes," Johnny said, "I think she would. And not because

she's, as you put it, fool enough, but because she gave this
old man her word. I think you've been brought up on a
mirage of the mind, if you think you'll find sacks of gold
pieces, waiting out there in a trunk. Give her the belt with
the key in it."

"Oh, please," Miss Opal put in. "If she'll be more satisfied carrying it in her bag, let her. I don't want to fight
about it. I don't know whether you're right or not about
the gold pieces, Cynthia. Maybe the poor man has hoarded
them. You're right, he did always use gold in business deals.
I remember his wife worrying about his always having so
much of it. 'It's real money,' he always said, 'whereas
checks, or oil stock are just pieces of paper.' " She passed a
hand bewilderedly over her forehead. "Come to think of
it, he did tell me not to try to carry the trunk myself, because it was terribly heavy. But listen, child, I don't want
the money. I told you he already gave me this cameo brooch
that was his wife's." She touched the brooch, pinned at her
neck.

Cynthia's lips curled as much as to say, "Not much you
don't want the money."

Johnny said curtly, "The fact remains that your Uncle
Jason gave Miss Opal the key."

"That's her story."

Again Miss Opal interceded earnestly. "I wouldn't beat
you out of the money, Cynthia. There's no reason why we
should fight about it. We can open the trunk together.
Will that satisfy you?"

"It'll satisfy me if I can carry the key."

"That'll be all right. If you'll take good care of it. Whatever gifts are in the trunk are marked, and I'll see that they reach the right folks."

Johnny turned to Cynthia. In all their years together, Beany seldom saw Johnny furious, so that from one rare time to another she forgot how flashing black and cold his eyes could be, how his face lost its genial boyishness and became grimly set like a man's. "It doesn't satisfy me," he said. "I think you're acting like a skunk, Cynthia. Miss Opal came to us and told us her story, honest and above board. You didn't. You came with a sad story of wrecking your car—"

"That was a lie, as Beany can tell you," Cynthia put in coldly. "I didn't have any car to wreck."

"I might have known it was," Johnny said with a bitter laugh, and Beany, with a flash of feminine intuition, realized that he was all the more bitter because he had defended her so warmly to Beany when she found fault with her. "But anyway, we made room for you. You've eaten Miss Opal's food. It reminds me of that old story about whoever it was who warmed a snake in his bosom and then it turned and bit him."

Cynthia didn't answer. But her stubborn face went pale under her tan.

Beany said uncomfortably, "I'll pack up our things so we can get going."

But Johnny wasn't through. "I only wish we didn't have to have you with us the rest of the way. If we had the money, I'd gladly give you bus fare and drop you off at the next town."

"To go home or go on to California?"

"I wouldn't care which. I'd take the key from you and part company with you."

"No, Johnny," Miss Opal said shakily, "we'll travel together and we'll open the trunk together. I don't want her to think I'm trying to beat her out of her rightful dues. . . . Come here, Martie pet, and let me wash your hands. . . ."

A car divided. This time when Johnny, his face still set in harsh lines, climbed into the driver's seat, Cynthia didn't maneuver to sit beside him. She climbed in the back to sit with Miss Opal. When Beany murmured, "We can take Martie up here," Johnny said, "No. He can sit in back. Then if he gets tired, he can stretch out and go to sleep." His tone said, "And you, Miss Cynthia, can like it or lump it."

A car of strained silence. Except for Martie's questions and Miss Opal's murmured answers. Except for Johnny's asking tersely of Beany, "Look on the map and see where there's a road that'll take us across to Highway Ninety-one."

"Ninety-one? But the fellow said we'd be safer from the road patrol if we stayed off it."

"I know," Johnny agreed heavily. "But the primary reason we're going to California is to deliver Martie to Elizabeth and Don. They're going on a cruise. They're waiting for us. We're only losing time, skulking along on side roads. We've got to take a chance on the police stopping us. If they do, and insist on taking Quaker—well, they do, that's all."

Another fifteen minutes of driving and Beany touched his arm. "Johnny, let me drive." she asked. She said it for two reasons. One, because Johnny's anger was still so great that he was driving at a reckless speed; another, because Beany's thoughts were milling about confusedly and she hoped that driving might help untangle them.

Johnny gave her a ragged smile of understanding. He stopped and changed places with her. Beany found the turn which would lead them back to 91 again. She guided the car in and out of mountains, across level stretches of plain. But her thoughts remained a tangle.

Supposing she turned and asked Cynthia, who sat staring out the car window, "Cynthia, what did Norbett have to do with all this?" What would Cynthia say? Suppose she asked directly, "Cynthia, was it Norbett who drove you to the town near Fort Bridger and put you up to telling you wrecked your car, so Johnny would take you in?" But she hadn't the courage to ask it. Maybe she hadn't the courage to hear the answers.

So Beany drove on, and Cynthia sat as though she were oblivious of them all.

In the late afternoon Beany wound around a shelf of a mountain road with a fertile valley showing below it. She strained her eyes to a clump of trees far ahead and muttered to Johnny, "Do you suppose there's a little town hiding under those trees? Look on the map and see if we're due to hit one in three or four miles."

Martie put in plaintively, "I wish we could get some ice cream."

Johnny was just fitting together the map, which had cut out at the folds, when Beany felt the car lurch as though a strong hand had given it a backward pull, and simultaneously came a gurgled scream of alarm from the back seat.

It was from Cynthia— "Stop—stop quick! The trailer—the wheel's rolling off—"

Even as Beany stopped, with a scrunching protest of brakes, a loose wheel went scuttling by her car door and rolled on merrily down the road. It wabbled uncertainly and fell on its side. An oncoming car had to slow and swerve around it. The driver kept on going, allotting the Malones only a curious and baleful glance.

Johnny was out of the car before it came to a complete stop, was loping down the road to pick up the runaway trailer wheel. Cynthia was out, too, speaking to the horse as he scrabbled frantically to keep his balance on the floor of the trailer, which was tilted far to one side. She was saying, "We've got to straighten the trailer—look, poor Quaker is all lopsided."

But the trailer, with its weight of horse, was too heavy for them to lift. Yet Cynthia couldn't back the horse out when it slanted so crazily. She was all concern for Quaker. "There, there, boy! I think he's bruised his neck. Oh, if we only had some help, maybe we could prop it up with a big rock, for a while anyway—"

Cars swished by. A few slowed, the passengers gawking curiously at their predicament, before speeding on.

And then a truck driver pulled his loaded truck up close to the mountainside and got out. A welcome sight, this burly fellow with his good-natured smile and perspiration marks describing a wide arch around the armholes of his blue shirt. Beany thought gratefully, It's always the truck drivers that think of the road as their home and extend the hospitality of it.

He took in the situation casually as though road mishaps

were nothing out of the ordinary, and said, "I got a heavy jack that we can put under the nub of the wheel and h'ist it up."

He brought the jack. He lent his broad shoulder along with Johnny's to lift the trailer, while Cynthia and Beany put the jack under it and in position. Johnny worked the handle of the jack and inched the trailer and Quaker to a level position.

Then they took cognizance of the situation. The truck driver shook his head portentously. "Looks to me like you got to get you a new wheel."

"Is that a town down there?" Johnny asked.

"Yeh, that's one of my stops, trucking out of Salt Lake. I can drop you off as I go through. Tell you who to go to see, and he'll treat you right. A fellow named Marve at the Super Garage. A lot of people are out to sock the tourists, but Marve won't. If you don't find him at the Super you go into the Elite Café next door. His wife runs it, and sometimes he's in there having coffee or giving her a hand. She's been kind of ailing lately. Gall bladder, I think. They're nice folks. I always stop at the Elite for coffee and pie. We can take your wheel in with us and let Marve have a look at it. Though it looks to me like the bearings are all ground out."

"But you won't be coming back this way?" Johnny asked.

"No, I got two more towns to make before I call it a day. But Marve can bring you back in his pickup truck." He took another look at the wheel; there was more man talk about lug bolts' being sheared off, about having to take off the whole drum. "Guess the womenfolks and the codger will be all right here till you and Marve get back." He started rolling the wheel toward his truck.

Johnny murmured ruefully to Beany, "Looks like this is going to shoot the rest of the day to smithereens."

Beany thought sickly, Looks like this is going to shoot the exchequer to smithereens, too.

Miss Opal spoke up hesitantly, "Would you have room for me to go on to the little town with you? I'd kind of like to."

"Sure," the truck driver said genially, "we can always make room for one more. Just leave my jack with Marve and I'll pick it up on my next stop."

So Beanie and Cynthia and young Martie were left on the mountainside to guard the car and Quaker. Cynthia eased the horse out of the trailer, examined the chafed bruise on his shoulder. "Do you think he's hurt?" Beany asked anxiously.

Cynthia was patting him, cooing to him soothingly, for the horse was trembling nervously. "I can't tell whether it's more than a flesh bruise or not." She walked him up and down the road, hugging close to the mountains. She stopped now and then to pat him or rub her hands along his neck. She got out the thermos jug and emptied it into a bucket, coaxed him to drink.

A long wait. It was hot in the car, and dusty with cars swirling by. Martie grew restless, plaintive. Not far away was a grassy spot where the mountain sloped toward the road and a tree cast a blotch of shade. Beany said, "I'll take Martie and see if he'll lie down there while we wait."

"Go ahead," Cynthia said shortly.

Strange that her voice was always gentle with the horse, Quaker, always curt to her fellow passengers.

Beany took the little boy up the slope and spread a blanket under the tree. She could look down on the car, even as she said to him, "Now lie real still while I tell you a story. Do you want to hear about Goldilocks' going to the bears' house while they were away?"

"Did she leave some peaches in a jar?"

"No," Beany chuckled ruefully. Her mouth watered in remembrance of those yellow peach halves suspended in syrup which they had left behind that morning for the unknown owners of the cabin. It seemed hours and hours since they had eaten Johnny's concoction, complete with almond meal, on pancakes. It *was* hours. They had stopped at eleven and it was almost five now.

Automatically she went through the story, with Martie correcting her on details, for her mind was on the money in the billfold which must last them till they reached Oceanside. They'd had three ten-dollar bills left after Johnny bought supplies for his memorable luncheon. One ten-dollar bill had been broken for the inevitable gas, and for repairing the windshield wiper on the driver's side.

She was telling about Goldilocks' enjoyment of the littlest bowl of porridge, when the little boy interrupted, "When are we going to eat?" and she thought, *What* are we going to eat?

Sitting there, she could look down and watch Cynthia walking Quaker up and down the road. A gray Ford with a Wyoming license slowed and a man in a Stetson hat looked curiously at the horse, and the trailer minus a wheel. He stopped and got out, leaving a woman, her hair wrapped in a green-flowered scarf, in the car.

He crossed the road and talked to Cynthia; he examined with careful concern the swollen spot on the shoulder which had grazed the top bar when the trailer lost its wheel and lurched to the side. Beany watched idly. She saw Cynthia tie Quaker short to the trailer so there would be no danger from passing cars. Cynthia and the man walked over to the car and talked to the woman.

Beany still watched idly as Cynthia came back to the Malones' Dodge and opened the baggage trunk and, with the man's help, dislodged two suitcases. Why, those were Cynthia's two—the two matching light ones with black stripes!

Beany got to her feet, twigs and grass still clinging to her seersucker. And then Cynthia came hurrying up the steep slope and said breathlessly, "He knows about horses. He said for you to get some Epsom salts and dissolve it in hot water—as hot as you can stand your hand in—and put hot packs on that bruised and swollen place night and morning. Fold a towel and put it on steaming hot. Do you hear? About fifteen minutes each night and morning till the swelling goes down. Johnny can hold him while you put it on—"

Beany repeated stupidly, "While I put them on? But you're better with Quaker than I am."

"No, you've got to do it. Because I'm going on. These folks—I knew their daughter in school. I'm going on with them. They're going straight through. You can tell Johnny I won't be taking up room in the Malone car any longer."

She turned then and ran swiftly across the road and to

the parked Wyoming car. It was only then that Beany remembered. She ran after her, calling, "Cynthia, you can't! You've got Miss Opal's key. Cynthia—"

But the Wyoming car with the man and his wife in the front seat, with Cynthia, suitcases, and woven pouch bag in the back seat, was already starting. Even as Beany screamed, "Cynthia—wait!" it glided surely and swiftly down the road.

And Miss Opal's key went with it.

15

SUPPER AT THE ELITE CAFE

It took Marve of the Super Garage an hour and fifteen minutes, after he arrived in his pickup with Johnny, to put into running order all those ground-out gears and sheared-off lug bolts which the truck driver and Johnny had discussed.

Marve was a wizened, black-eyed little man who looked as though he had been sautéed, clothes and all, in black grease. And while he wielded odd-shaped monkey wrenches, while he lay on his back under the trailer to tighten all the innumerables which needed tightening, Beany told Johnny about Cynthia and her sudden taking off in the gray Ford with the Wyoming license.

"I keep wondering what I could have done," Beany regretted. "But it all happened so fast. She just said, 'I'm going on with these people,' and she was down the road and opening the car door before I remembered the key and

yelled after her. I don't know whether she heard me or
not."

"She heard you all right," Johnny said grimly.

What could she, Beany, have done? Even if she had run
after and caught Cynthia, they could hardly have fought
for possession of the red belt with the key sewed in it in
the middle of, or at the side of, the highway.

Johnny asked, "Ford, eh? New?"

"Pretty new. Maybe a year old." It grieved Beany, somehow, to see Johnny's twinkling eyes so hard with disillu-
sionment—Johnny, under whose picture in the yearbook
at Harkness High had been printed, "With Malice Toward None."

She was even relieved when the small Martie, who had
been hunkered down watching Marve and conversing
with him, came over and took Johnny's hand and said, "He
says they're having chicken for supper at the Elite Café
and he asked me if I liked drumsticks and I said I did. I
told him I could eat three."

Johnny swung the small figure up on his shoulder. "I
guess you could, Punk. And three would be just an ap-
petizer for me. Soon as Marve's finished we'll hustle right
down and dig up some supper."

But they would have to dig carefully because of their
diminished funds. Beany asked, "Do you know how much
Marve's going to charge, Johnny?"

He shook his head. "The suspense is terrible, but we'll
have to wait till we get back to the Super Garage and he
figures up the cost of parts. And his time, driving up here
and back, as well as working on it."

The sun was sinking fast when Marve finally straightened up, gave the wheel a testing kick or two. He gathered up his tools, tossed them in his faded red pickup, wiped his hands on a bit of black waste, and said, "I'll see you down at the garage."

He drove off.

A sober Beany and Johnny Malone loaded Quaker back into his remodeled house on wheels and, with Martie between them, set out for the little town to pick up Miss Opal —and food. The amount of food depending on the amount of Marve's bill.

Marve was behind his desk figuring it when they stopped at the Super Garage. Miss Opal, he told them, was next door. More fidgety suspense as Marve added a long row of items. He thrust the itemized bill at them. They bent over it. Beany knew a great relief. It could have been so much more. Nine dollars and eighty cents.

Beany was just putting the twenty cents' change from a ten-dollar bill back in their funds when Miss Opal came in, staring hard to locate them in the oily-smelling gloom of the garage. Her cheeks were flushed, and the transparent green cellophane apron she wore changed the shade of the lavender tulips in her dress to a sickly hue.

She said happily, "I've been helping Marve's wife in the café. Her gall bladder's been bothering her, the poor soul. I've baked nine cherry pies since I got here. So you're all to come in and have supper. Marve's wife—I can't remember whether it's Della or Stella—said for me to give you a hot, filling meal. We're having chicken and dumplings or baked ham and— Where's Cynthia?"

Even as Johnny, she made little comment when Beany told of Cynthia's hasty leave-taking. She only leaned heavily on the rack of tires and made small tch-tch-tch sounds. Beany noticed that her ankles were swollen more than usual from her hours of pie-making.

It was only Beany's self-reproach that she answered. "Why, you couldn't have done a thing to stop her, lovey, not a thing! As for the key—well, if she's dead set on getting to the trunk, she could do that without a key."

"I only wish I'd taken that key away from her," Johnny rasped out.

"Now, now, we'll not fret about it," Miss Opal went on. "We'll all sit down at a table and eat a good home-cooked meal. And I was inquiring from Marve's wife—it's either Della or Stella—about our getting a cottage camp for tonight. They're all pretty high in the tourist season but she —come to think of it, I believe it's Bella—called up a friend of hers that runs one called Shady Rest, and she'll let us have a room with one double bed and a single for three dollars and a half. That's the best I could do."

"The best!" Johnny said with a tired flash of smile. "You did superb to earn us our supper. It's chicken for mine. But I've been wondering if we couldn't drive on after we eat. We could watch out for that gray Ford with a Wyoming license. And if we catch up with it, we'll have your key for you."

Miss Opal considered it, her eyes on Martie, who was at the water cooler, trying to unflatten a flat paper cup without much success. His blond hair, which usually formed a soft halo about his head, was flattened limply. He looked so small and woebegone as he stretched to the water tap— his Levis well down on his hips as though there wasn't enough little boy under them to hold them in place.

"No," she said firmly, "the little fellow's tuckered out. Might be I could give him a bath after supper. And you'll want to dose up the horse as Cynthia told you. No, other things are just as important as my business of Mr. Jason's trunk. We can get an early start in the morning."

Beany burst out impulsively, "Miss Opal, you always think of everybody else—"

Miss Opal only tch-tch-tch'ed at that remark. "Now come on in. I figured twenty minutes on the dumplings and they ought to be just right." She took out her handkerchief, wet it in a trickle of water, ran it gently over the little boy's face. She rubbed it over his grimy hands and said, "Come along, ducky."

It was a good thing Marve's wife—whether Stella, Della, or Bella—was unstinting. Never had chicken, dumplings, and green beans been dispatched as swiftly, or as appreciatively, as those set before the Malones. Johnny had three helpings of everything before he sat back, sighed, and reached for the warm cherry pie.

"I told Marve's wife I'd do the dishes and for her to go to bed," Miss Opal said, stacking up plates.

"You'll do nothing of the kind," Johnny said, taking them out of her hands. "You'll take yourself and Martie off to bed. I'll do the dishes while Beany does up Quaker."

Beany went in search first of a feed store to buy oats, then of a drugstore and the Epsom salts for treating his bruise. The town's only feed store was closed and dark. She could find only a creamery which was still open and which carried some canned goods and staples on its shelves.

They had no large cartons of Quaker Oats. Only a smaller size. A gray-haired woman handed one to Beany and she turned it over in her hand and read, "Wt. 1 lb. 4 oz. Net." The price was nineteen cents. "It's for our horse," Beany confided, "and he'll need a gallon. I wonder how many of these it would take."

The woman recited, "A pint's a pound, the world around."

Beany computed that. A pint's a pound. A pound was a pint. Two pints in a quart, four quarts in a gallon. Eight pints to make a gallon. If this carton contained a pound and a fourth—which was a pint and a fourth—then you'd divide that into eight.

The woman obligingly found a pencil and they both figured on a flattened sack.

$$8 \div 1\frac{1}{4} = 8 \times \frac{4}{5} = \frac{32}{5} = 6\frac{2}{5}$$

Oh heavens, it would take more than six packages for Quaker's supper tonight.

"What time does the feed store open in the morning?" Beany asked smally, thinking of Quaker's breakfast.

"Lew's feed store? Oh, Lew gets down around eight thirty, quarter nine sometimes."

"We'll be leaving town earlier than that," Beany mused worriedly. "I think six packages, without the two fifths would do. I think twelve packages for supper and break-fast would do. Twelve times nineteen cents—" She figured it twice, hoping that two dollars and twenty-eight cents wasn't right. But it was.

The woman said magnanimously, "I'll tell you what, honey. As long as it's for a horse, I'll let you have all twelve for two dollars."

"Oh, thank you," Beany said gratefully. "Thanks a lot."

Next stop the drugstore. Beany parted with sixty-nine

cents for the large economy-size Epsom salts. She trudged
with her load to the Shady Rest cottage court, tried not to
think as she shook out the six cartons of oats to Quaker,
"There goes a dollar. . . ." And Mary Fred had said
blithely, "He won't be any trouble. . . ."

Their room at Shady Rest had no kitchen accommoda-
tions. She had to go back to the Elite Café, where Johnny
supplied her with hot water. He offered to carry it for her,
but she said, "No, finish up your pots and pans. I can
manage."

This treating of Quaker's bruised shoulder was a job
Beany didn't relish. But she mixed the Epsom salts in the
steaming hot water. From her grip she extracted a towel;
it was fragrant smelling from the soap Kay had given her
and she, in turn, had given away to the unknown owners of
the cabin.

Gingerly, fearfully she applied and held the hot, moist,
folded towel to Quaker's injury. He fidgeted, of course,
and Beany found herself talking the same soothing horse-
language Mary Fred and Cynthia did, "There, there, boy
—I wouldn't hurt you. Steady now—that's the fellow. Got
to get this swelling down before we deliver you to
Ander—"

For fifteen minutes she worked with him. And then,
with the satisfied feeling of a job well done, she fell into
bed beside the sound-asleep Martie.

16

QUAKER EATS ON THE BORDER

The sun was high and hot at seven the next morning when they departed from Shady Rest and eased back onto Highway 91. Added to the luggage in the back seat was a wrapped cherry pie which Marve's wife had given them as a parting gift along with her, "Now be sure and stop on your way back."

The desert lay ahead of them. The landscape grew more arid and barren, the air more oven hot. Beany opened the car door and held it ajar with her foot, hoping the swirl of air would cool the car. The water in their radiator steamed, then, as the speedometer checked off the miles and the sun lifted higher, boiled and bubbled over with abandon.

Toward noon they stopped at a filling station at Las Vegas. The attendant took one look at their gurgling radiator and reached for the water can.

Beany climbed out of the car, said, "Whew, it's hot!"

The man answered conversationally as he poured water down the radiator's steamy throat, "Hot? Today isn't so bad. There's a little breeze today. Now yesterday was really a dinger. A car drove up here, and stopped right where you're stopped, and a woman got out and she stood right there where you're standing, and all of a sudden—plop!—she went down in a heap. Dead."

Beany moved hastily out of the ill-fated spot.

Johnny said, "I guess it'll be pretty hot driving the desert. Some folks were telling me it's better to lay over here and drive it at night when it's cooler."

The man's only answer was a grunt as he set down the water can. He picked up a chamois to wipe the rusted shower from the radiator off their windshield. "Wish I had a nickel for every banged-up car that's been towed in here from this night-driving the desert. Oh, sure it's cooler! But the catch to it is that the road's like a ribbon, and the fellow behind the wheel dozes off. Just one split second is all it takes."

They drove to a little square of park in the center of town. They spread out blankets. Again they invested in bread and lunch meat. In ice cream for Martie. Oranges to quench their thirst on the drive. Oh, and they mustn't be caught again without oats for Quaker. Beany said, "Try to find a feed store, Johnny. It's cheaper than buying him breakfast food."

Johnny found a feed store and returned with a bulging gunny sack. "Sorry, Beany, but he wouldn't sell me less than fifty pounds. But at a gallon a feeding, he'll soon go through it."

"Don't ask me to figure gallons and bushels," Beany said.

The park was filled with townspeople and travelers. All of them wilted. Babies cried fretfully and old men dozed. The water fountain was ever circled with thirsty people.

They sought a patch of shade under a tree. But the shade didn't feel like shade. The sun was too insistent to be held at bay by foliage.

Johnny queried dubiously, "What do you think? Would you rather wait here till the afternoon is half over and tackle the desert in the cool of evening, or hit it hot in the middle of the day?"

"It couldn't be any hotter than this," Beany said. "At least we'd be moving. This air presses down like those hot driers in a beauty parlor."

And so, after filling the thermos jug, the radiator, Quaker, and themselves with cool water, they set out. The road led them on, confidently wide and boulevard smooth through patches of desert, through mountains.

"You always think of mountains as being cool," Beany mused, remembering the crisp, piny air of the Rockies, and the rivulets which coursed down their sides to make ice-cold springs from which travelers drank. But these mountains which broke the desert lacked vegetation. They seemed to have been molded of hot lava which stayed hot.

"They have their own inner heating system," Johnny said.

They didn't speak about it, but Beany could sense the alert watchfulness of Johnny and Miss Opal as well as herself, every time a pearly-gray car showed ahead of them. Was it a Ford? Did it have a Wyoming license? Was it driven by a ruddy-faced man in a Stetson with a woman wearing a flowered green scarf beside him? And was there a dark-haired girl in the back seat?

They saw gray Fords. They saw Wyoming licenses. They even saw gray Fords with Wyoming licenses and speeded up, until Quaker in his trailer swayed perilously behind them, only to find the car driven by a vacationing school-teacher, a college boy, or a family man with the back seat crowded.

"Seems fair enough," Johnny commented wryly. "We haven't caught up with a gray Ford, and the road police haven't caught up with us."

More dun-colored desert with dunes rippling like pictures of ocean waves. Mirages of lakes and lovely green trees. And closer at hand, large billboards advising, "Stay Awake with No Doze." Filling stations bore signs, "Please don't ask for radiator water. We haul our water fifty miles."

Beany and Johnny spelled each other driving. Beany's bare arm, which she rested on the open window ledge, was burned cerise and was sore to the touch. Miss Opal fumbled through her Mother's Helper and found a lotion which temporarily soothed. She also found some Life-Savers, which helped keep Martie content. They sucked oranges. Again and again they tilted the unwieldy thermos jug and drank from it.

They stopped at a hot little town for water for the radiator and for Quaker. The descending sun cast down scorching rays. This time Beany backed Quaker down the runway of his trailer with comparative ease while Johnny got the water bucket. This time Beany led him up it again and tied his halter rope, and gave him a comradely pat or two.

They faced into a blinding sun. Beany had to hold the partially folded and battered map in front of Johnny's eyes as he drove. And suddenly it was sunset on the desert. Rolling sand dunes of coral. Why, Beany thought, does something so beautiful make your throat ache? Then—as swift as stage-shifting—they were lavender with purple shadows. They were gray with black shadows.

And, as suddenly, it was night. "And miles to go before I sleep." Johnny was driving. The last time Beany had looked at the map there had been some three fourths of an inch between them and the town of Barstow, California. But Beany knew now that a fraction of inch on the map meant miles and miles.

The air that fanned through the car had a caressing, lulling coolness. The whir of the wheels was soporific. Beany thought of the filling station man's saying, "Wish I had a nickel for every car that's been towed in here from this night-driving the desert. . . . Just one split second is all it takes."

"Johnny!" she broke the silence. "Are you sleepy?"

He lifted his drooping head and shook it hard. "Let's sing," he said desperately, "and if you don't hear my off-key bass, nudge me hard."

They sang. Old songs, new songs. Beany's eyelids grew heavier. Those sand dunes at the side of the road would be cool now. If only they could pull up someplace and lie down and feel the give of sand to their tired bodies. But the road constantly warned, "Soft Shoulders." There was nothing to do but keep going.

Then Beany started a guessing game. Who could name the most song titles with a girl's or boy's name in them?

Miss Opal gave the old ones. "I'll Take You Home Again, Kathleen." "Danny Boy." Johnny and she came in with the newer ones. "Irene." "Margie." "Rose, Rose, I Love You."

Johnny burst out with forced vigor, "I dream of Jeanie with the light brown hair—"

There flashed through Beany's mind a scene as vivid as though she were seeing it on a movie screen. A foursome in Downey's Drug. They had been attending a high-school Literary Club meeting and were crowded into one of Downey's booths eating chile. Beany could see one girl clearly, objectively—not as though it were she, Beany Malone, but another girl, young and naïve and so hopeful that her red-headed escort would like her in the white wool jersey with the blue belt and blue slippers her sisters had loaned her. How those pumps of Elizabeth's had pinched her feet! After the chile when others ordered ice cream the girl (she had her pumps off under the table) had ordered blueberry pie. And the boy had broken into lusty song, "I dream of Beany with the light blue teeth. . . ."

But that was so long ago. Was Norbett singing now, "I dream of Cynthia with the dark brown hair?"

Johnny broke the nostalgic spell. "Here, kid, you better take over before I go to sleep at the switch."

Beany drove on through the night. It gave one an eerie feeling, this following a road on which a dark and mysterious land fell away on both sides.

And then suddenly she felt her hackles raise in fear. A strong waving light a short way down the road focused on them, waved in a circle, caught them again. Johnny roused, said, "They're motioning us to stop. Slow down, Beany."

"What is it, Johnny?" Her heart was pounding hard. Was it a holdup? Was it the police still watching for the Colorado car with horse and trailer attached? No, it must be an accident which blocked the road for, as Beany came on warily, she could see a dark mass of cars.

"Bless us and save us!" Miss Opal breathed under her breath.

A uniformed man held the high-powered flashlight which motioned them to pull in and stop behind another car. He muttered something about "inspection center."

It came to them then. This was the station where their car and they would be checked before crossing the California line. Wearily, groggily, yet relievedly Johnny and Beany alighted from the car to await their turn. First an examination of drivers' licenses, of car ownership.

They answered no to all the questions, "Any fruit? Any vegetables? Any seeds? Any of your belongings packed in straw or grasses?" The flashlight played over the back seat where Martie slept, his head in Miss Opal's lap. Over the cushions, blankets, the carton containing the coffee pot, skillet, and a remaining jar of chokecherry jelly, the green box of Epsom salts.

They opened the luggage compartment of the car, and there the flashlight found the sack of oats which Johnny had bought in Las Vegas. The fifty pounds which was to last Quaker until such time as Ander took him over. "Oats, huh?" the officer said. "You can't take that across the line."

"We can't!" Beany said strickenly.

Other travelers had told them about the restrictions on fruits and vegetables because California guarded against possible plant diseases. They had made sure to eat every orange, but they had never once thought about the oats. "But we'll need it for Quaker tonight. You see, we haven't got much money and we just bought that in Las Vegas—"

"Sorry, miss, but we'll have to confiscate it."

"What'll you do with it?" Johnny asked.

"We might cook it up for porridge," he said airily, "or make a bonfire out of it."

"Oh no," Beany said. She asked, "We haven't reached the state line yet, have we?"

"No, not quite but—"

"Then, look," she pleaded desperately, "let us take out a feeding for him first. He'll eat it right away. We should have fed him about sundown but we kept putting it off till we'd stop someplace."

He scratched his chin dubiously, and Miss Opal thrust her head out of the car window to say, "Oh, I'm sure he'd be kind enough to let a hungry horse eat some first. He wouldn't take away his supper."

The fellow chuckled. "Okay, miss. I've never had this come up before, but I guess there's no law against oats' going across the line if they're packed in a horse's stomach."

Beany heaped the gallon measure high; she even scooped up a half measure extra, and whispered fiercely to Quaker, "Eat it—eat every bit of it." And eat it Quaker did. He was still champing appreciatively and tonguing a few extra grains from the corner of his mouth when Beany put him back in the trailer, which Johnny had been ordered to sweep out with a broom lest any grains cling to the floor.

And at last it was their turn to be waved on. When they finally reached the town of Barstow it was night and they

were too weary to hunt about dark, unknown streets for
the least expensive lodging. They made one stop at a small,
lighted grocery and bought two cans of soup. They drove
on slowly until they saw an electric sign spelling out the
word "Vacancy" before a cottage court.

Six dollars for a room with only one double bed, a
kitchen the size of a telephone booth, a dripping shower!
But they dared not demur because the woman kept muttering, "I don't know about renting to folks with a *horse*."

They opened the cans of soup. But their stiff weariness
was greater than their hunger. Johnny disengaged the
front seat from the car, folded blankets on it for the little
boy. He pulled off his sleeping bag for himself.

Automatically, wearily Beany heated water and swirled
the white powder about in it till it dissolved. Quaker stood,
docile and submissive, when Beany held the hot, wet towel
to the swelled spot on his shoulder, as though he sensed
that Beany had pleaded in his behalf.

She held the dripping towel in place and sagged her
weight against the horse. And he accepted it, nuzzling at
her gently as though to remind her, "We are born to bear
the weight of humans." Beany murmured, "Quaker,
you're nice—I'm sorry I called you an albatross."

She continued to lean against his solid bulk while her
eyes half closed, while she thought wearily, Tomorrow
we'll count the money we have left—and figure the miles
—and figure some way to stretch it. Tomorrow will be
time enough—

17

CALIFORNIA, HERE WE ARE!

The last day. The last lap of the road. "Look. travelers,"
Johnny said, spacing off the road on the tattered map with
his thumb and index finger. "Look at how far we came
yesterday. We've only got about half that distance between us and Oceanside today. Why, that's duck soup.
Whoopee!"

The last day. The last lap. About a hundred and fifty
miles. Duck soup.

It would be duck soup if their remaining three dollars
and forty-two cents held out. Oceanside, the oasis, the goal.
They could telephone Elizabeth from there. And Ander
would be waiting for them at a cottage court with a blue
trim. Blue Haven. Ander would promptly send off his
check to the irate once-owner of Quaker. Ander would
promptly repay them for their investment in the trailer,
and for Quaker's expenses en route. Including the price

198

of this morning's purchase of twenty-five pounds of oats.

"We'll be opulent," Johnny said. "We'll be those rich Americans you hear about."

They bought a big box of crackers, which they spread with chokecherry jelly and breakfasted on, along with a thin cocoa which Miss Opal made out of a Hershey bar she unearthed when she rummaged through her Mother's Helper for needle and thread.

Highway 91 led them through picturesque and verdant country. For the first time they saw trees polka-dotted with yellow balls which were oranges or lemons or grapefruit. They passed roadside stands, colorful and tempting with arrays of fruits, the names of which they didn't even know. "How I'd like to make the acquaintance of a kumquat," Johnny murmured. They passed by stands where moist, glistening dates were sold—and drove on, eating crackers and washing them down with water.

It was while they were feeling their way through traffic in a bustling town called Victorville that another car drew up alongside them and the driver leaned out to inform them, "Hey, your left rear tire is pretty low."

They drew into a filling station. They had to buy more gas to finish the trek anyway. "Six gallons ought to take us there," Johnny computed. They hadn't counted on oil, but the attendant held up for their inspection the slim, black, and oily rod from their oil case. "Pretty low," he commented.

"We got oil yesterday," Johnny said.

"You drove the desert yesterday, huh? Well, that burns up the oil."

"Okay, put in a quart."

The attendant also diagnosed the left rear tire as having a slow leak. "Probably your inner tube." Inner tube, or outer tube, Beany thought grimly, we've got to worry along with it. They filled it with air and drove on prayerfully.

After that it was a regular chore, stopping at stations and filling that left rear with air which gently oozed out as they drove.

By now there was a veritable network of roads so that the map resembled a jigsaw puzzle. They had to leave Highway 91, and it was like parting from a friend who had constantly given them a reassuring smile. Beany had to scan the map closely each time they came to a branching of roads or an intersection.

From force of habit they still craned their necks at sight of a gray car which might, upon closer inspection, prove to be a Ford with a Wyoming license and, at still closer inspection, have as a passenger, Cynthia Hobbs. Yet by now each one said to the other, "Oh, those folks have probably seen most of California by now." And each one thought, "Cynthia has probably seen what her Uncle Jason left in his trunk by now."

The constant stops to have air put into the left rear tire gnawed into their time. And the worry of whether the gas and oil and the miles and their funds would come out even gnawed at their consciousness. Elsinore. Temecula. The slow leak was not so slow by now. They had to stop oftener. And still helpful people drew up alongside to announce to them, "Your left rear's low." As though it was news! And Johnny, the courteous, would smile his thank you.

When, in the middle of the afternoon, little Martie's, "When are we going to eat something besides crackers?" became a distressful plaint, Johnny said resolutely, "Criminy, we might as well be flat broke as the way we are. How much dough we got, Beany?"

Beany emptied the small jangle of silver into his palm. Two quarters, three dimes, two pennies. Johnny took it and came back with a hamburger apiece, and a frozen ice-cream stick for the little boy. He held out the remaining two dimes. "Twenty cents—twenty miles left to go," he said. "I'll drive, you pray."

Beany did pray, sitting taut on the edge of the seat, her eyes on the gas-tank register, which had long since passed the quarter-full mark. The upper half of the zero was flirting coyly with them when they came into Oceanside's city limits. "Now watch for the cottage camp trimmed in blue," she reminded Johnny, and Miss Opal and Martie as well.

They passed one cottage camp. There was nothing blue about it.

They were approaching another, set back in an oasis of trees. It had a garden spot at the side filled with painted furniture. Beany suddenly clutched Johnny's arm. "Johnny, look there—look—"

"Is it trimmed in blue?"

"No—but look, sitting on that green seat. Look, Miss Opal—it's Cynthia, isn't it?"

Johnny stopped with a jerk and simultaneously two things happened. The left rear tire gave an exhausted, beaten whish-sh, and the corner of the car dropped a good two inches. The other happening was that large

drops of rain, without warning of clouds or thunder, pat-
tered down.

The girl at whom they stared was sitting, or rather
slumping, on a green bench. They identified her by the
two pieces of matched luggage, and her striped sweater
and rumpled green skirt. And her dark hair. They couldn't
see her face for her arms were crossed about her middle,
and she was bent over as though in pain.

As they walked toward her, she raised her head and
stared at them out of heavy, dark eyes. Miss Opal spoke
first. "Cynthia, are you sick?"

She only nodded. Even her lips were gray white.

Beany asked, "But where are the folks—your friends
from Wyoming that you went off with?"

"They've gone on," she said in a labored monotone.
"I told them I only wanted to go as far as Oceanside.
They let me off here early this morning."

"They shouldn't have gone off and left you like this,"
Miss Opal said reprovingly.

"I wasn't sick then. I guess I ate something. I guess it
was the chile I got in a little Mexican restaurant this noon.
It tasted funny—when I ate it—but it was cheap and I
—I was so hungry." She turned her head in deathly nau-
sea.

"Sounds like ptomaine," Miss Opal said. Cynthia's teeth
set up a weak chattering, and Miss Opal added, "Come
on, Cynthia, and I'll get you to bed. Warm soda water and
lots of it—"

"I haven't any place to go."

Johnny had only stood there without speaking. He said
now, "We can't get any farther because our tire's gone

out. We'll see about renting one of these courts and then you can come in and Miss Opal will take care of you."

Again Cynthia raised her dark eyes to look at Johnny. Beany thought for a second that she was going to say, "You mean you'd take me in after what I did?" But instead she said flatly, "They won't rent you a place without paying in advance."

"They won't," Beany said heavily.

"I'll go in and talk to them," Miss Opal said.

She was gone a long time. Johnny moved a striped umbrella over to shelter them from the gentle rain. No one spoke. Cynthia's woven pouch bag lay beside her on the bench. It would have been so easy for either Johnny or Beany to reach for it and extract a rolled-up red belt. But it would seem—well—almost unfair when Cynthia was lumped over in pain, uncaring and defenseless.

Miss Opal came out of the office and walked slowly toward them. She had a key in her hand and she said, "I finally got number 67, clear down at the end."

Johnny flashed her a grateful grin. "Miss Opal, the miracle-worker! Is this cottage court trimmed in blue, by any chance?"

Miss Opal shook her head absently. "No, sort of a heliotrope, or maybe fuchsia—"

Beany noticed that Miss Opal's hand fluttered to the collar of her dress where no cameo brooch was pinned. The plump, veined hand was shaky, and Beany said, "Miss Opal! You left them your cameo brooch—but you shouldn't have. You'll feel lost without it."

"No—no, that's all right. I left it for a deposit—and my, the woman was pretty uppity. No, what I'm wondering about is if we can't get to the end motel without going right past the office. Yes, I think that you can keep on the main road, Johnny, and turn in at the far end so they won't see us. I don't mean *us*," she added more worriedly, "I mean the trailer and Quaker."

"Why? Doesn't the uppity woman like horses?" Beany asked.

"I think they've been told to watch for us."

"Oh-oh! The road police and the dragnet!" Johnny's lax figure stiffened. "What did they say?"

Miss Opal said apologetically, "My ears are still sort of hummy—they get that way in the mountains and it takes a few days for them to clear. But while I was talking to the woman—and, oh dear, she was pretty uppity about letting us have a room!—her husband came in, and I just caught the words Malone and horse trailer, and watching out for them."

They stood in uneasy thought. Beany muttered, "Gee, we've brought Quaker all this way—" and Johnny added, "And Ander's practically got his hand on his halter. We've got to hang onto him a little longer."

Miss Opal contributed, "So I signed the register in my name, Miss Opal Macafee, and I put down Arvada, instead of Denver, because that's where my little farm is. And I never breathed the word Malone—"

Johnny said, "Our license plate is so dust covered, no one can read it easy. I noticed it those times we stopped for air. It'll take a harder rain than this to wash it off. If we just had a pocket big enough to put Quaker in." He hesitated a frowning moment, looking up and down the busy street, and then said resolutely, "We'll unlatch the trailer. We just passed a car lot and I'll ask them if we can leave it there for a short time—"

"With Quaker in it?" Martie asked.

"No. Quaker can slide in on his own four feet. You see, if we drove in, unattended by a trailer, we'd be just another car. They wouldn't think a thing of it. Or they wouldn't think anything of it if they saw someone go loping down the road on a horse—"

"Who's going to lope down the road on a horse?" Beany asked thinly, even as she knew the answer.

"Who do you think?" Johnny grinned. "But you can take your choice, Miss Malone. You can either drive the car on a flat tire or ride the roan nag."

"I'll ride him," Beany said, "but don't expect me to lope."

Cynthia had only listened wanly to their discussion, only contributed weakly, "I'd ride him—if I wasn't so —so woozy."

"You come and get in the car," Miss Opal said, taking her firmly by the arm and helping her to her feet.

And thus the Malones, in broken and camouflaged formation, took over their unpaid-for motel quarters in what Johnny termed Heliotrope Heaven. Beany went first on Quaker, trying to act as nonchalant as though she were out for an afternoon ride, trying not to hang onto his mane in tenderfoot fashion when he broke into a happy canter.

Johnny followed with the car, bumping and lurching on its flat, *sans* the trailer. "We'll hide Quaker in our garage space," Johnny said, "and with the car in front of him, he won't be visible to the naked eye."

Even before they fitted the key in the lavender door they were awed by the exterior. "The Monterey influence," someone murmured. Stucco walls of cream color, tile roof. Window boxes painted that same pinkish lavender, in which flowers of the same shade obligingly bloomed.

Miss Opal took a hasty look about the interior. "My goodness, tiled kitchen and bath—and did you ever see such a big, lovely room? I'm afraid it's pretty swanky for us."

"Beggars can't be choosers," Johnny said.

"There's a purple sink-drainer and a clothesline outside," Martie imparted.

Beany stared in uneasy pleasure about the surprisingly large and lovely room. Two double beds, two chests of drawers, easy chairs, benches and desk in blond wood. Everything matched or blended in shades of lavenders, corals, and blues—the draperies hung at windows with Venetian blinds, the bedspreads, the leatherette cushions on the chairs. A splashy picture of the desert, done in those same shades, greeted them from the wall.

Miss Opal was all clucking concern over Cynthia. A limp and docile Cynthia submitted to her ministerings. From the Mother's Helper Miss Opal produced some soda, stirred it into a glass. "If you can just get everything up, you'll feel better. Beany, put a pan of water on, and maybe later she'll feel like a cup of tea."

It was while Beany was opening cupboard doors of knotty pine, looking for a pan to boil water in, that she found a sack which some previous tenant must either have overlooked or decided wasn't worth carrying on. Three potatoes and a large onion with a slice taken off it. She held them up jubilantly. "Now I know how Robinson Crusoe felt when he found—what was it, now—a cask that washed ashore?"

Johnny's eyes brightened. "We can make clam chowder without the clams. Life is looking up. I'm setting forth to find a garage man with a heart of gold who'll trust us for an inner tube and some gas on our promise to pay as soon as we locate Ander Erhart and become solvent."

Beany threw off her lethargy of weariness as she peeled potatoes and that one huge onion, sliced them, and put them on to simmer.

She moved softly, conscious of Cynthia's sickness. Who could harbor vindictiveness for a girl who had to clench her teeth on her whimpers? Beany even knew reluctant admiration for her. Once, as Cynthia came out of the bathroom swaying on unsteady legs, Beany took her arm and guided her to the bed. Miss Opal helped her into bed, wiped her perspiring face with a washcloth, murmuring all the while, "There now—there now, you'll feel better once you get it all up."

A relieved Cynthia lay limp and pale.

Johnny returned and, in answer to Martie's anxious, "Did you find a garage man with a gold heart?" grinned ruefully. "No, just a career girl with a hard chromium finish around hers. I went to this big garage down the street but got no farther than Miss Stonyheart in the office. No cash—no inner tube or gas. But guess what, I shopped around and bought this chunk of fish—identity unknown—with our two dimes. We'll cut it up in slivers and add it to our chowder."

They divided the chowder into four bowls; Cynthia

only shook her head sickly when Beany asked her if she could eat a little. She could take only a few teaspoons of the tea Miss Opal brought her in a coral-colored pottery cup. "A whole set of Monterey dishes," Miss Opal sighed. "Dear, dear, I'm afraid the rent on this place will be pretty steep. I was so rattled while I was in the office I didn't ask the price."

Beany's fears ran along parallel lines.

It showered and stopped, showered and stopped. During an intermission Beany went to the office of the motel court to put in a call for Elizabeth in San Diego. She could ask the operator to reverse the charges.

The woman who sat behind the motel switchboard must be the "uppity" one Miss Opal had mentioned. Her gray hair was precisely waved, and she was laden with Indian bracelets, necklace, and earrings. Beany stood an uneasy moment, while the woman completed a call, and her eyes roamed about the office.

Above the switchboard desk was an enlarged camera shot of a stocky, middle-aged man riding across plains that looked like those in Colorado or Wyoming. Glancing out the glass door Beany saw a stocky, middle-aged man— who was evidently the man in the picture—tilting up the painted lawn furniture so that the rain would drain off.

He came hurrying in, carrying two pots of lavender flowers. As he placed them on the wide window-sill Beany offered conversationally, "Those are pretty flowers."

"Yeh. Though I don't know yet what you call them." He smiled at Beany with a folksy twinkle. "She—" indicating the woman at the switchboard—"stood over a painter for three days so his paint would match them when he painted the doors and trim."

The woman turned questioning eyes to Beany. Beany said, "I wanted to put in a phone call to my sister in San Diego. She's Mrs. Donald McCallin, and this is her telephone number. And I'd like to reverse the charges, please."

"And what is your name, please?" the woman asked, plugging in a cord.

"Beany Ma—" and then she checked herself. She mustn't use the word Malone. She stammered, "I'm her sister and we—"

The woman said crisply, "I have to have your name to give the operator so she can ask the party if she'll accept the charges."

Beany said flusteredly, "Well, I—I believe I'll come back—later on—"

The man interceded, "You don't have to come up here through the rain to telephone. You've got one in your apartment."

"We do? Oh, I didn't see one."

"It's in a sliding panel over one of the beds. All the conveniences of home—and then some. You can put in your call to us from there. And we'll ring you when we get your party."

"Well—thank you—" Beany said, and hastily departed in the rain and dusk.

Sure enough the telephone was revealed when Beany slid back a blond panel. "Dear, dear," Miss Opal murmured again, "there's even a let-down ironing board in the kitchen. I never dreamed we'd live in such style."

"To which we are unaccustomed," Johnny added.

They looked at the telephone sitting there, so smug and proper in its niche. And so useless to them for telephoning Elizabeth. For it would only connect them with the woman at the switchboard in the office. And they couldn't put through a call and ask to have the charges reversed without giving their name.

Johnny sighed. "We've got to comb the town over for a cottage court trimmed in blue where Ander awaits us."

"But not until the rain lets up a little," Miss Opal said.

A time of waiting. Beany curled up beneath the telephone on the bed in which Martie was already sound asleep. Of waiting till the rain slackened so they could set out in quest of Ander. Of waiting till Miss Opal put their accumulation of soiled clothes to soak in the bathtub; then Beany meant to wash her dusty hair. Of waiting till Cynthia felt better, and could drink the cup of hot tea which Miss Opal prophesied would settle her stomach.

The rain drummed on, on the tile roof.

Beany wakened in the middle of the night. Someone had pulled off her shoes, covered her. She sat up in bed and looked about in the dark. In one bed Miss Opal and the weak enemy slept. And that dark blotch she could see on the tiled floor of the kitchen must be Johnny in the sleeping bag. It was still raining. Everyone slept relaxed, like wilted plants soaking up the moisture.

Beany's mattress between the headboard and footboard of blond wood was soft as a cloud. She straightened out Martie's humped-up figure, fell into heavy sleep again.

18

EVEN A LAVENDER SPONGE

When Beany went into the kitchen the next morning, Johnny was stirring something in a pan on the stove. She bent over to look at and sniff the thick, bubbling mixture. She gasped out, "Why, John Esmond Malone, you're cooking some of Quaker's feed-store oats!"

"Oats is oats, my sweet. And if we find a few sprigs of alfalfa or some millet seed—" He broke off, his spoon stilled, and eyes blinking in rapt concentration. "That's it! Why didn't we think of it before? The telephone call to Elizabeth. I'll give the name John Esmond, without the Malone. That won't mean anything to the folks in the office, but it will to Elizabeth. Here, Beaver, stir this."

Thus it was that within five minutes Elizabeth's voice was saying in such loud excitement that all those standing about could hear every word, "John Esmond Malone, why all the formality? The operator lost off the Malone but I knew— Oh, Johnny, where are you—how are you—when did you get in?"

Johnny said, "Here, I'll let Beany give you the gory details while I stir the porridge."

Beany took over the telephone to hear, "Beany, you blessed, I'm so relieved to hear from you." For a minute Beany thought she was going to cry at the sound of that warm, familiar voice. She had to swallow twice before she answered smally, "We're at Oceanside, we got in late yesterday afternoon, and we wanted to call you but—" No, she'd better not go into that. The uppity woman at the switchboard might hear.

Elizabeth hurried on breathlessly, "I've been hugging the phone for days and days. Are you all right, honey?"

"Yes, we're fine."

"What kept you so long?"

"We couldn't make very good time. We brought out Ander's—" No, she'd better not mention horse. That, too, might be incriminating if it were overheard.

Elizabeth didn't seem to notice any gaps in the conversation. "And how's our Martie?"

"He's fine, too. He's right here. He wants to say hello."

She put the little boy to the telephone and he promptly shouted, "Hey, Mommie, I want some caps for my gun."

Elizabeth was still chuckling when Beany took back the telephone. "Beany, we'll come up just as soon as we can get there. Although Don isn't here now. He's been dismissed from the hospital for about a week, but he had to drive out today for his final examination and dismissal papers. I'll have everything ready and we'll come the minute he gets back. I'll bring a picnic lunch. Is there anything special you'd like to eat?"

Just *anything*, Beany thought, but she said, "You know how Johnny likes chicken."

Elizabeth's laugh could be heard by everyone in the room. Miss Opal murmured, "Oh, it's wonderful the way the Malones can laugh."

Beany had to ask often, "What did you say, Elizabeth?" for Martie was prompting her, "Tell her the caps are like teeny-weeny lumps in paper and you tear them off." Johnny was nudging her, whispering, "Don't let on to her that we're subsisting on horse food and hope." And, in the background, Miss Opal was all bustling activity. "Martie, pet, you've got to get that cowboy shirt off so I can wash it."

Beany turned from the telephone to say, "Somebody quick hand me one of those match folders so I can give her our exact address." Elizabeth wrote it down, said, "We might be held up by Don being held up at the hospital, but we'll be there as soon as ever we can with enough food for all five of you— Oh, and, Beany, I'm bringing a nice young man for you, so look your prettiest and be your sweetest to him."

"Oh! What's the young man like?" she faltered.

"He's the kind you should go for—if you don't I'll shake you. Oh, sweet, our time is up. Don't worry if we're a little late—you know how army hospitals are."

Even as Beany replaced the telephone in its blond niche, Miss Opal was saying, "And she's bringing a nice young man for you! Now you wash your hair the first thing."

Cynthia contributed, "I have some shampoo cream you

can use." She tugged her suitcase out of the closet, dropped down on one knee to open it. She was wearing the gray and pink gingham but there was no pink in Cynthia's wan cheeks to match the pink of the dress this morning. She handed Beany the jar of cream and Beany said self-consciously, "Thanks a lot, Cynthia."

"We're like the poker player," Johnny said. "We got prospects. Chicken coming up. So line up for your oats. They're strengthenin' and fillin'. Slightly more palatable, of course, if served with milk or cream."

Cynthia let out a happy gasp. "Look—I was folding my tan jacket, and I found this in the pocket. A quarter I didn't know I had. I'll take it and get some cream."

"Milk will go farther," Johnny said. "Here, give it to me. My legs are longer and stronger than yours. You still look on the fragile side."

Later when Beany piled the empty bowls in the sink and Cynthia had walked slowly out to see Quaker, Beany asked Miss Opal, "Did you say anything to Cynthia about the key to Mr. Jason's trunk?"

"No—no, lamb, I didn't like to mention it."

Beany appealed to Johnny, "Don't you think Miss Opal ought to ask her for it?"

"I'd rather not," Miss Opal said gently. "She's been sick. She seems so—so unlooked after. I've always believed that no one is really bad. It always makes me happier to trust someone and let him live up to it. I feel sure that Cynthia has changed."

Johnny said generously, "I don't see how she could keep from it. Gosh, Miss Opal was up and down with her most of the night, stepping over me and my bedroll here in the kitchen. I figure it like this: our Cynthia gal never had anyone who did for her. Anything her parents did for her was only trying to outdo the other set. No, I think Miss Opal's right and we shouldn't get heavy with her about the key."

"And besides," Miss Opal added, "anxious as I am to tend to the trunk for Mr. Jason, I won't worry about it until we get Martie's clothes washed and ironed before his folks come for him. Did either of you see the other red-striped sock like this?"

Johnny set forth to look for the cottage court trimmed in blue, and Ander who would be waiting.

Beany washed her hair. She used the mirror over a chest of drawers for twisting it up in tight little snails and spearing each one to flatness with a bobby pin, for Miss Opal was busily sudsing clothes in the bathroom. Cynthia sat watching her. Once Cynthia began falteringly, "Beany, I've just been thinking—"

She didn't finish her sentence because just then Johnny opened the door and Miss Opal left her washing to ask him, "Did you find Ander's cottage court?"

"No, and I walked all the way to the beach. But I've got an idea. We'll slip Quaker out of his hiding place and walk him down through the streets—or maybe you'd ride him, Beany?"

"We'll walk," Beany said quickly.

"Put on your swimming suit. We'll take little Martie and anyone else who wants to go. If Ander is looking for Quaker, he'll be more apt to see him parading about than poked back there behind our car. And another thing," Johnny added, his brown eyes bright with enthusiasm, "when I was at the beach I saw a fellow giving his horse a bath in the ocean. And did that horse love it! I got to talking to the fellow and he said it was as good as a shot in the arm—if a horse had an arm, that is. I told him about Quaker and our lugging him all the way from Colorado in a trailer, and he said a salt bath would be just the thing to limber him up."

"Do you suppose Quaker would like it?" Cynthia questioned.

"Sure," Johnny said. "You ought've seen that horse stick his nose down in a big wave that came along. I told the fellow about the bruise on Quaker's shoulder that's just about well, and he said salt water was the most healing thing in the world. He said for us to sponge ocean water over the bruise and pat it in."

"We haven't got a sponge," Beany said.

"Ah, but we have! I noticed one last night under the sink."

Johnny was right. There was a rectangular cellulose sponge for the washing of the Monterey pottery dishes, and even it carried out the color scheme in being a bright lavender. Once again Miss Opal murmured, "Oh dear, I wish they didn't have everything so perfect."

Johnny wadded the sponge in his Levis pocket, said, "Be nice to have old Quaker all shine and prance when we turn him over to Ander, won't it?"

"Yes," Beany assented, carried along, as usual, by Johnny's contagious enthusiasm. So was Miss Opal enthusiastic, although from a different angle. Getting the small Martie into his swimming suit was one way of getting him out of his cowboy shirt while she mended, washed, and ironed it.

"Come along," Johnny said. "Big Ears can play in the sand while we work on Quaker. Want to come too, Cynthia?"

Cynthia hesitated and Miss Opal answered for her, "I think she'd better take it easy for a while yet."

Through the caressing, fragrant California morning Beany, Johnny, Martie—and Quaker—walked down Oceanside's streets. Once Beany stopped, and the procession came to a halt. "Johnny, I just remembered. Elizabeth said she'd bring plenty of food for all five of us. How did she know about Miss Opal and Cynthia?"

"I don't know. Maybe you mentioned it yourself. You two were talking at such a high lope. Come on. At the next turn you can see the ocean."

It was Beany's first sight of the ocean and she stood for a few breathless moments, thrilled and awed and frightened by its immensity. . . . Now why, why should she suddenly wish Norbett Rhodes were standing beside her? Was she doomed to go through life thinking of Norbett at every high and exalting moment? . . .

"They copied it from picture post cards," Johnny said. "And did a nice job, didn't they?"

Quaker seemed far more frightened than thrilled by the expanse of water and the waves which rolled in, broke harmlessly on the beach, and eased out again. As they led him across the sand and around the scattered sun bathers, he went on wary, reluctant feet, snorting and pulling back on his halter rope.

"He'll like it once he gets the feel of it," Johnny said confidently.

They settled Martie to digging in the sand and hunting

sea shells. Johnny rolled his Levis knee high. Beany dropped off her seersucker skirt, carefully adjusted the swimming cap which matched her yellow suit so that her bobby pins would not prick through it.

With Beany tugging hard at the halter and coaxing, with Johnny behind slapping and urging him onward, they coerced Quaker into shallow water, which lapped upon the wet sand and his fetlocks.

Johnny extracted the purple sponge from his pocket. He was just lifting it, dripping with salt water, and Beany was cautioning, "Start easy, Johnny—he's trembling all over. He doesn't care much for this—"

With that a wave, higher than any preceding one, came in with a roar and a splash. It would have caught Quaker on the chest except that he reared straight up on his hind legs in snorting panic, whirled, knocking Johnny and the sponge aside, and bolted. Beany looked down at her empty hands. They were still clenched from holding the halter rope which had been yanked through them.

A few scattered people on the beach tried to head him off, tried to turn him back. But there was no turning back for Quaker. The folks could only step aside while Quaker's hoofs splayed wet sand, then dry sand. They lost him from view behind a hamburger stand with wide awnings.

The life guard sauntered up to them with an amused grin on his leather-brown face. "Dry land horse, huh? They don't cotton to the ocean."

"We thought it'd be good to limber him up."

"He don't need any limbering up," he said laconically.

Beany hurried to gather up her skirt and button it over

her wet swim suit. They gathered up Martie and started after the horse.

Yes, different ones told them, they had seen a roan horse go by. "And he wasn't stopping to pass the time of day." They walked up one street, down another. The small Martie hampered their speed. First Beany would go ahead, then she'd take Martie's hand while Johnny's long legs hurried on. A man cutting his lawn saw the horse turn east up there by the filling station. A boy on a bicycle saw a roan horse, with halter rope dangling, turn west there by the white house. A woman at a fruit stand said he stopped and nibbled at an apple in the street and then went on.

For hours they walked and asked. And finally Beany said wearily, "Let's take Martie back to our motel. He can't walk any farther."

It seemed a long trek back to their motel. Martie's short legs gave out entirely so that Johnny was carrying him piggyback as they came to where the crescent-shaped road led past the row of low stucco apartments and their own lavender door with 67 on it.

Johnny stopped for breath. Beany was looking ahead to the office at the other end of the curving drive. She gasped out in unbelieving relief, "Quaker's home. Imagine that —he knew enough to find his way home. See up there in front of the office. And there's Ander—that is Ander, isn't it? Yes, it is!"

"It's Ander in person—unless some other cowpoke has a green checked shirt just like Mary Fred gave him Christmas. But who's the woman with him and Quaker?"

"I don't know," Beany said bewilderedly. "It looks like the uppity one—only she's smiling at us."

Beany was even more bewildered by all that transpired in the next ten minutes. At Ander chuckling and saying, "Imagine me, riding down the road, coming to ask Mrs. Fergus here if my Colorado folks had arrived yet, and seeing a roan horse nibbling grass along the roadside."

"He got away from us," Johnny panted, swinging the burden on his back to the ground. "We were giving him a bubble bath in the Pacific so as to have him all shined up for you—if and when we—"

The woman interrupted; it *was* the uppity woman but now she was all hospitality and apology. "Oh, I'm sorry, but I didn't know that you folks were the ones we've been looking for for days. Because the woman who came in and registered didn't mention the word Malone. She didn't say a word about your having a horse or I'd have—"

Ander interrupted her. "I've been at a dude ranch about twenty miles out, and they put on rodeos every afternoon and I've been doing exhibition roping. But every morning I'd come breezing in to ask if the Malones and Quaker had arrived. And then you come slipping in, secret as top-drawer—"

Beany had to interrupt. "But we thought it was the road police and we were afraid to say we were the Malones. They tried to stop us in Utah—a truck driver told us so —because the farmer didn't want us taking Quaker out of the state."

"Why, no," Ander said positively. "The farmer who owned Quaker was peaceable as pie. He telephoned my father when the horse wasn't on Barberry Street and Dad

sent him the money right away. Dad telephoned me out
here and told me about it."

"Oh!" was all Beany could say weakly, puzzledly. . . .
Could the truck driver have only imagined that the road
patrol was inquiring about a '41 Dodge with a Colorado
license, and horse trailer attached?

Ander said, "You must have had trouble along the way?"

"A little," Johnny temporized. "We were scared of the
police and thought we'd duck them by getting off the main
highway—"

"And then a wheel rolled off the trailer," Beany put
in. "And, Ander, if you go back the way we came, you stop
at the inspection center and ask them for that fifty pounds
of oats they took away from us. It broke my heart."

Ander threw his arm around her. "Beany, you're a
trump. I wish I didn't have to leave you but I have to get
back to the ranch and the afternoon show. But I'll be in
in the morning. You still like caramel sundaes? I'll buy
you all you can eat."

"Me, too?" Martie wanted to know.

"You, too," Ander said. "I've already got a hitch on
my car for the trailer so I can take Quaker back with me.
Want to get him broken in to roping. Is the trailer here?"

"We left it up the road a little ways," Johnny said.
"Come on, and I'll go with you."

Beany said, "Ander, wait! You told us to stop at a cottage court trimmed in *blue?*"

"Well, isn't this?"

"Oh no!" Johnny said. "Look, guy, if you call this
blue, what color does that make Beany's eyes?"

The owner of the motel laughed indulgently. "Ander,

Ander! After I labored to grow petunias this certain
lavender shade and wrangled with a painter for a week
until he got a perfect match. You better stick to your
roping—don't ever go in for dress designing."

Beany patted Quaker's forehead with the blurry, upside-
down seven on it. Imagine Beany Malone feeling a pang
of regret at parting company from a *horse!*

Ander and Johnny and Quaker walked off in the direction of the car lot and the trailer, leaving Beany and Martie
standing beside the motel owner. Beany said, "Mrs. Fergus,
just as soon as Ander pays us what we paid for the trailer
we'll pay you for our motel."

"You'll not pay us a cent," the woman said positively.
"You are our guests. Why, we go to the Erhart ranch for
a month or six weeks every fall for my husband's vacation.
He and Ander's father went to school together. Any friend
of the Erharts is a friend of ours. You stay as long as you
can. We just hope you're comfortable. I'm sorry if I
seemed inhospitable yesterday—but if we'd only known.
If there's anything else you'd like, you just tell us. Oh,
and here, my dear, give your friend back her brooch."

Beany took two or three deep breaths before she could
say, "Well, thank you—thank you. No, there isn't a thing
more we want."

She tugged at the little boy, anxious to push through
their own door at number 67 and announce to Miss Opal,
"Don't worry another second about the Monterey pottery,
and the telephone in a wall panel, or the sliding ironing
board—or even the lavender sponge."

But Martie got through the door ahead of Beany to
announce loudly, "Hey, Miss Opal, she gave us back what

you wear under your chin. And we can stay as long as we want—we're guests."

Miss Opal was lying on the bed. She sat up, looking startled and flustered. "My goodness," she said, blinking and rubbing her flushed face, "I didn't intend to drop off. I just thought I'd stretch out a minute to rest my feet. It must be the change of altitude, but they swelled over my shoes so bad while I was ironing."

Beany glanced about the room. All about it was evidence of Miss Opal's labors. Martie's open suitcase full of clean, ironed, and folded clothes. The desk top was covered with Johnny's T shirts and underwear, which had been ironed to dryness. Beany's own white dress, freshly pressed, hung on a hanger. "Why, Miss Opal," Beany reproached. "You shouldn't have done all that. You should have waited till I got back."

"To tell the truth," Miss Opal confessed, "I thought I'd better hurry. I didn't know but what we might be put out any time, because that uppity woman acted as though she didn't think that brooch of mine was worth much. What are you saying lovey?" she asked as little Martie kept repeating, "She gave it back. Tell her, Aunt Beany."

Beany told her of the events of the morning, ending with, "And if there's anything else we want, we're only to ask for it."

Miss Opal said simply, "Ah, God is good. That does take a load off my mind."

The room smelled strongly of perfume. Beany looked about. "Where's Cynthia?"

"Isn't Cynthia back yet? The poor child must be having trouble getting it fixed."

"Getting what fixed?"

"Your car. She said she was going over to see the girl at the garage that Johnny said had a heart of chromium."

"Did she drive it over? On that flat tire and without any gas?"

"Yes, she did. Or maybe she got a little gas—I don't know. She was sort of in and out. Let me see, I was pressing your white dress and Cynthia looked at it and said she had a white dress. She said it cost a lot of money and everyone was crazy about it. And then she got it out of her suitcase. My, it was pretty—though no prettier than yours. Some perfume had spilled in her suitcase, and Cynthia stood there, holding the gold sandals that matched the belt, and worrying about how perfumy the dress smelled. I told her to put it on the line to air, and then I'd press it for her to wear at the picnic supper tonight."

Oh no, Beany thought. Cynthia in that white dress, gold belt, gold sandals would be too remindful of another evening.

"She went out with it," the placid voice continued. "And then I guess I—like the doddering old thing I am! —fell asleep. What time is it now?"

"It's after two," Beany said. "We spent so long hunting for Quaker when he got away. You go ahead and rest some more. You've worked so hard—and you were up and down so much last night."

"That's what Cynthia told me. She told me to rest while she looked around and saw what she could do about getting the car fixed."

Beany left Martie in the motel and went out. Yes, the

car was gone. She walked down the sreet to the next block and across to a big and busy garage. Perhaps Cynthia was inside seeing about their leaky flat. Cynthia would be glad to hear that Ander and Quaker were reunited at last.

Beany stepped into the office and the first thing her eyes lighted on was Cynthia's white sun-back dress. It was hanging on a hanger which had been wrapped with white paper, and was protected carefully from dust or smoke by a green transparent raincoat. The gold sandals sat on the floor under it. Each one of them had a sheet of onionskin paper tucked around it.

A slim, efficient girl finished a column of figures on the adding machine before she turned. Beany said, "I'm looking for Cynthia—the girl—well, that's her dress."

"It's mine now," the girl said, and her eyes, behind their glasses, lighted with pure feminine, acquisitive joy. "Isn't it a love? It's nylon, and an original, and I've just been dying for a dress like that. I'm going to wear it to a rodeo performance about twenty miles from town tomorrow. They usually have dances afterwards."

"But where is Cynthia?" Beany asked.

"Oh, she's gone. She came in and showed me that dress and sandals, and asked me if I'd trade her an inner tube and a tankful of gas for them. And I did."

"Where did she go?"

The girl shrugged. "She didn't say exactly. She said she had some business about twelve miles out of Oceanside. She was in quite a rush. She's been gone for three—maybe four hours now. You know, I couldn't have had sandals fit me better, if I'd gone down and tried them on. And the dress smells strong of perfume—it's Shocking by Schiaparelli—and that's always been my favorite. The dress was just a little snug, but then I tried it on over this—"

Beany walked out on the young woman's pleased chatter.

19

REUNION

As Beany walked back to their motel through the hot, sultry afternoon, her rage mounted with each step. So the wily Cynthia had maneuvered to get their Dodge fixed in order to sneak out to where her old Uncle Jason had left the trunk—in order to rifle it without benefit of Miss Opal.

She couldn't wait to tell Miss Opal and Johnny. Those two, with their high-sounding talk about trusting a person. Those two, thinking the leopard could change spots —*had* changed spots because the she-leopard had given Beany shampoo cream, and donated a quarter for milk to pour over the feed-store oats they had breakfasted on.

Beany pushed through the door of motel number 67. She had to blink a minute in the dim light for Miss Opal had half closed the Venetian blinds. Johnny had returned. He said, "Beany, behold! Strike-it-rich Johnny, they calls

227

me." He fell into an ecstatic ballet step, tossing something resembling green leaves into the air and catching them as they fell.

"Sh-h," Miss Opal cautioned, motioning toward the small hump in the corner bed, "don't waken the little fellow. I want him to be rested when his folks get here."

Beany saw then that the "green leaves" were ten-dollar bills. Johnny explained softly as he stopped to pick up one off the floor, "From Ander with his undying gratitude."

"But there're so many," Beany said in a hushed voice. "That's more than you and I put in the trailer. My thirty-eight and your twenty-two were only sixty. Mary Fred put in forty-eight."

"He's already sent Mary Fred her ante. I fought like a steer when he shoved these ten ten-dollar bills in my hand. I told him it was too much and wouldn't take them. He got positively wrathy about it. He said it was paying us back for our money, plus Quaker's feed and the repair to the trailer—and our mental and physical duress. So he crammed them into my pocket and leaped in his car and yelled back that he was making plenty on his roping exhibitions."

"It was worth it to him, and he wanted you to have it," Miss Opal soothed. "My, everything is turning out so nice. I was telling Johnny about Cynthia and her taking the car to see if she couldn't get it fixed up for you folks."

Beany opened her mouth to say, "Not for us—for Cynthia," but Miss Opal was asking, "Do you think it would be too soon to put on water for coffee, Beany? I even found paper napkins with Mexican designs on them."

Miss Opal was all bustling anticipation. Everything in the room had that same pleased getting-ready-for-company gleam to it. Their clean, dress-up clothes laid out. The opened gate-leg table held plates, cups, silverware. So festive, so partyish.

Beany remembered the older woman's hurt shakiness that noon in the mountains when she found that Cynthia had preëmpted the key to the trunk. I can't tell her, Beany thought, but I'll tell Johnny.

Johnny gathered up the bills, smoothed them and pressed them into Beany's hand. "I'm considering getting my hair cut for the reunion so Elizabeth won't make dirty cracks about tying a pink ribbon on it. Or maybe I'd better go find Cynthia. I hate to think about the poor gal getting the dust-off the way I did last evening when I begged for extended credit. What do you think, little Mom?"

His very calling her "little Mom" sent a rush of protectiveness through her. Johnny of the warm heart, the high heart. Johnny, so sincere and chivalrous and generous and guileless that trickery would always be a blow to him. Johnny, too, had seemed so un-Johnnyish that day when he had told Cynthia that she was like a snake which, after being warmed, had turned to bite. . . . Beany remembered suddenly her own pain when she had found out that Norbett, whom she trusted, had deceived her. . . .

She said decisively, "You go get your hair cut, Johnny. Because—well, I guess Cynthia would rather you didn't go looking her up."

Johnny said as he went out the door, "I also considered buying us each a hamburger, but I figured it would be better to disgrace ourselves by falling on Elizabeth's food like wolves. Can you wait?"

"I guess so," Beany said flatly.

"They ought to be here soon," Miss Opal said. "Beany, you hurry and get ready. Here's your white dress. You'll want to look pretty for the young man Elizabeth is bringing."

Beany hurried. Now I can start forgetting Norbett, she told herself as she clasped Mary Fred's silver belt around her waist. This hollow, sick feeling inside me is hunger, she told herself as she slid tanned feet into Mary Fred's sandals. Cynthia and Norbett are two of a kind, she told herself as she ran a vicious comb through her curled top-knot and pinned up her braids. . . . "Don't you cut your hair," Norbett had said. "Braids and Beany go together. . . ." If I had time I'd whack them off now, she thought bitterly.

And when her lipstick was on and Miss Opal said, "I knew you'd look sweet in that dress," Beany said restlessly, "I think I'll go out—and watch for them."

But it wasn't the McCallin car from San Diego she wanted to watch for. It was their own dusty Dodge with Cynthia in it. She wanted to stop her, tell her that she, Beany, knew of her treason. She wanted to say, "But I'll cover up for you till the party is over. I'll save Johnny and Miss Opal that long."

She had hardly reached the end of the crescent-shaped driveway when she saw the car she was looking for. Cynthia had slowed for the traffic to clear before she turned in. Beany yelled out, "Cynthia, wait!"

Cynthia stopped and got out of the car. Her dark hair was mussed. One tanned arm had a scratch on it. The rumpled skirt of her pink and gray gingham had an L-shaped rent in it. Cynthia said wearily, "I thought I'd be back before you missed me. Beany, did they find out—Johnny and Miss Opal, I mean—that I got the car fixed and went to find the trunk?"

"No, they didn't. But I did. I went to the garage and the girl there told me you had urgent business outside of Oceanside."

"It was only twelve miles and I thought I could get out there and back before you folks hardly knew I was gone. And I could have only that trunk is so heavy. Oh gosh, I tugged and tugged at it but I couldn't even lift a corner of it. So I had to drive another five miles to get a couple of men to lift it in the car for me. Then I had to take them home again. I guess I should have told Miss Opal, but I wanted to surprise her—and Johnny, too. But when it took so long, I realized what a dumb thing it was—that they might think I sneaked off to open it so as to get the jump on Miss Opal—"

"Didn't you?"

"No. I wanted to get it so we could open it together. She was busy and tired and I thought I'd save her that much. I left the key in the belt in one of the drawers at the motel. Is that what you all thought—that I—I was acting like the snake Johnny said I was like?"

"That's what I thought. But what else could I think?" Beany flared. "The girl at the garage said you came in and traded her your dress and sandals and that you were in a great hurry to go twelve miles out of Oceanside."

"Did you tell Johnny and Miss Opal what the girl at the garage said—and what you thought?"

"No, I didn't."

"You didn't?" Cynthia said slowly. "I wouldn't have blamed you if you had. Why didn't you?"

"I don't know." Beany lifted her two hands, began kneading them together in front of her. "I wanted to. I went hurrying back to tell them—and then—then—"

"Then what, Beany?" Cynthia prodded.

"Then—well, I remembered how it hurt to find out that somebody—somebody you thought wouldn't lie to you—" Her voice broke, and a tear fell onto her clenched hands.

"Beany, don't cry—please," Cynthia said swiftly. "Honest, Beany, I almost told you this morning—maybe I would have, only Johnny came in. I was a skunk about the whole business," she went on incoherently. "It wasn't Norbett's fault—the poor guy. But you hated me so, Beany—when I walked into the cottage court back there near Fort Bridger—you're such a bum actor! I could see how furious you were because Johnny said he'd take me with you. Oh, maybe I'd have been mean and let you go on thinking what you did anyway—I don't know, because I've always gotten a kick out of giving girls a bad time if I got a chance—"

"But it was you that Norbett—I heard him begging you not to go to California. I heard him begging you to go back with him."

"Listen, Beany—blow your nose first—" She even reached over and wiped Beany's eyes and repeated earnestly. "Now listen. He wanted me to go back with him because he didn't want me to go with you folks and make trouble about the trunk. No, wait and I'll start at the beginning. I was all ginned up about Uncle Jason's leaving a trunk full of gold pieces. And Norbett thought it'd make a whale of a story. 'Rich Old Eccentric Leaves Wealth in

Gold Pieces. Old Woman Tries To Dupe Young Heir' and all that stuff. I couldn't talk to him at the Park Gate because my father always thought it was a lot of malarkey when Mother or I talked about our rich Uncle Jason, so Norbett took me—"

"To the Ragged Robin," Beany filled in. "I guess you told him about Miss Opal and how unscrupulous and mercenary—"

"Oh yes, I gave him the works, because I believed it myself. And I made him vow, even before I told him, never to breathe a word of it. Beany, I don't believe there're any gold pieces in that trunk. I—well, it was that night out at Fort Bridger that I began having doubts—and so did Norbett—only I was so stubborn I wouldn't give in. He put in a call to some reporter friend in Denver to check up on Miss Opal's story with the doctor and nurse. And I found out, as I rode along with all of you, that Miss Opal wasn't the kind to get around a sick old man."

"She's so good," Beany murmured.

"And she sees good in everyone," Cynthia added soberly. "I guess it was her believing that even I was good that made me want to do something decent for a change. And Johnny —Nothing ever went so deep as his saying I was like a snake that somebody warmed in his bosom and then it turned and bit him. All the time I rode with those Wyoming folks, I kept thinking of that."

Beany stood with Cynthia by the roadside while traffic swirled by. Rising above all the hodgepodge of her emotions was sick regret and self-reproach. She had been so ready to condemn Norbett. And now it was too late.

A car honked behind them long and arrestingly. Beany

looked back to see Elizabeth opening the car door, running toward them. She hugged Beany and said all in one breath, "Is this the welcome committee? It took Don so long at the hospital. Oh, this must be Cynthia. You two go ahead in your car and lead the way and we'll follow."

And then motel number 67, was given over to the hubbub of reunion. Introductions. Everyone talking at once. Beany moved through it dazedly. Cynthia nudged her. "Beany, you tell them the trunk is here."

Beany said as though she were speaking a piece, "Johnny, Cynthia went out and got the trunk so we could all open it here. She wanted to save you the trouble, Miss Opal."

Cynthia said, "You'd better unsew the key out of the belt. It's right there in the top drawer."

Miss Opal said, "Why, lovey, that was nice of you," and Johnny said, "You got the car fixed, huh! Well, you're a better man than I am. But then you have charm."

Dazedly, Beany accepted the packages, the pans, the cartons that a pale and limping and smiling Don McCallin put in her hands. Someone—it must have been Miss Opal —said, "The trunk can wait better than our stomachs can. Bring it in, and we can sit on it while we eat. We'll open it afterwards."

Someone, it must have been Johnny, said, "Hey, where's this dazzling man for Beany we been hearing so much about?"

Elizabeth had dropped down on the bed with the wakened but bright-eyed Martie on her lap. She looked up from pulling on wisps of red socks. "He'll be along any minute. He stopped to buy some picture post cards. Beany, you look ravishing. Someone ought to bring in that drippy ice-cream freezer and set it in the sink. I made ice cream right after I talked to you folks. Had to borrow the freezer from our landlady. Peppermint-stick. Because I remembered how Beany liked it, and was always making it."

You're wrong, Beany's heart contradicted. It was Norbett Rhodes who liked it, and that's why I was always making it.

Elizabeth added, "Beany, why don't you go to the end of the driveway and show—show your date where to turn in."

Beany muttered, "I'd better see about the coffee," and went into the kitchen. She stood there beside the gurgling percolator and, while the bustle eddied about her, felt only desolation. Peppermint-stick ice cream! It wasn't fair to fill her with this ache of nostalgia for the Beany who made it and the Norbett who ate it, grinned his appreciation at her, and said, "All this and heaven, too." Look your prettiest and be your sweetest, Elizabeth had told her this morning. She didn't want to look pretty for or be sweet to a strange young man. It was a familiar young man she wanted.

Somebody bumped into her and a voice said, "Gangway —before I drop this freezer on your toe."

Beany's eyes lifted to the tall boy who belonged to the voice, who deposited in the sink a freezer with crushed ice and salty water spilling over. Unconsciously she flattened herself against the stove until, feeling the heat and steam of the boiling coffee against her back, she backed away a few steps and felt the cool enamel surface of the icebox against it. She couldn't even say, "Hi, Norbett," for she scarcely had enough breath to breathe with.

She heard Johnny's glad voice. "Norbett Rhodes, as I live, breathe, and sometimes eat! What are you doing out here?"

Norbett answered, "I figured I might as well come the rest of the way as long as I got a good start. And—well, I was kind of worried about—things. Thought I might catch up with you. But I lost you. I've been down with Elizabeth waiting for a couple days. I—I hope I'm not horning in—"

Cynthia reached for a platter out of the cupboard. She said, "I wouldn't call it horning in. I've told Beany the whole sad story, Norbett. So you won't need to grovel too low."

Norbett muttered, "I don't know of anyone I'd rather grovel to."

And still Beany couldn't think of the right—or even the wrong—thing to say. Then Miss Opal was gently herding them into the big, noisy room. "Everyone take a plate and fill it. Here, Beany, you and Norbett sit right down here on the trunk."

Side by side they sat, balancing full plates on their knees. Beany was conscious of their all watching her. It was bad enough never having privacy for a fight—but how could you say the things your heart wanted to say when all those fond eyes were on you, those fond ears listening? Beany ate chicken and it might have been bologna; she ate peppermint-stick ice cream and it might have been lemon custard. They spoke only trite nothings.

Miss Opal was telling about their trip, "And we started

out with a tomato plant in a bucket. But Martie fed the tomatoes to Quaker—"

Johnny broke in loyally, "And Cynthia nursed him through his subsequent colic."

"—and so I just left it with Mattie Leavitt near Fort Bridger. We can pick it up as we go back." Under cover of an extra hubbub, occasioned by Martie's trying one of his new caps in his pistol, Miss Opal leaned over to say for Beany's and Norbett's ears only, "I left something else with Mattie, too. A bracelet I found on the ground. That is, I tucked it in the dirt the tomato was growing in. I didn't think it would hurt it."

Beany's heart beat hard and slow. She said catchily, "Well—thanks, Miss Opal."

"It's silver," Norbett said briefly. "It's come through a lot, that bracelet."

Martie was prompting, "When are we going to open the trunk? I want to see all the sacks of gold."

Beany and Norbett vacated their low seat. Beany nervously dusted off potato-chip crumbs. It seemed to take Miss Opal a long time to unsew the key which she had sewed so tightly on the inside of the wide red-velvet belt. They crowded about while she turned the key. The lid creaked on its old hinges as she opened it.

There on the top, in a man's careful writing, was the list of its contents and the names of the people he wanted them given to. A mechanical-drawing set, which had come from Germany, for a boy who was working his way through architectural school. A toby jug for a former landlady who was collecting them. A sheaf of letters his wife had written him; those he wanted destroyed. His wife's wedding dress.

Mementos of trips. An old dueling pistol to go to the curator of a museum.

"And here's something for his great-niece, Emily Cynthia," Miss Opal said.

Cynthia opened it. "It's an old singing book. Look how long it's been in the family. Look at what is written on the flyleaf, 'To Jason Hecht, for being a good boy and coming to singing school.' And look at the date—1840."

"Maybe the old fellow knew you were interested in singing," Johnny said.

Cynthia held the book, turning its old pages with gentle, thoughtful fingers. "You like it, don't you?" Martie asked with a child's discernment.

"Yes," Cynthia said soberly, "it makes me feel like part of a family—roots, sort of. I've never felt it—exactly—before."

At the bottom of the trunk, they found what made the trunk so heavy that Cynthia had had to drive five miles to get two men to load it into the car. It was not sacks of gold pieces, but great stacks of photographic plates. They were labeled, "Plates of pictures taken in Utah and Colorado by my father from 1850 to 1888. For anyone who is interested in the history of that time."

Johnny let out a long-drawn whistle of appreciation and excitement. "Who will you give *them* to, Miss Opal?"

"Why, Johnny, if you can use them, you're welcome to them. I know he'd want you to have them."

"Can I use them! Why, I'd rather have them than diamonds. I can use the Utah ones for my Jim Bridger paper. And Norbett, here, would only give ten years of his life for some of the early Colorado ones. His *Tribune* is going to run a big anniversary number and he has been grieving because everyone else has combed the state for any and all early-day pictures."

Norbett had picked up one. Reverently he held it up to the light. His voice was awed. "These are finds. These were taken about as early as ever a camera clicked."

"You can use some of those and, with a slick story to match, you're sure to get a by-line in the anniversary number," Johnny said happily.

Beany added, "And then you'll be promoted to juicy murders."

The creaking lid was finally closed on the trunk. "To-morrow I'll follow out Mr. Jason's wishes," Miss Opal sighed.

Norbett reached in his pocket, drew out a sheaf of bright-colored post cards. "I got these for you, Beany. I remembered that you wanted to send some to your friends and say, 'Having a wonderful time. Wish you were here.'"

Beany asked, "Can I use your pen?"

"Just a minute. I have to write one first."

He wrote swiftly and then, while the others in the room talked back and forth, slid it in front of Beany. The card was addressed to Beany Malone, Oceanside, California. The message read, "Have had a miserable time. Glad you are here."

Beany reached for a card, addressed it to Norbett Rhodes, Oceanside, California. Her message was, "Me, too. I'm sorry I was so—" Her pen hesitated over the right word. Norbett took it from her hand and filled it in, "Beanyish." He even added, "I don't blame you."

It was all so silly, yet Beany's heart lifted with each word.

It was like old times in typing class when, under the watchful eyes of the teacher Norbett called Miss Motto, they typed messages back and forth.

Elizabeth said, "Beany, write a card right away to Father, and we'll send it air mail."

"I will," Beany assented.

But she had one more message for Norbett. She turned the card over and wrote across a blue sky over a picturesque mission, "Life isn't charmed without your charm bracelet." Norbett barely found room to add to that, "Me, too."

Elizabeth was saying, "Father was so worried about you. He came home that Monday after you left. He found out about the extra money you had to pay for the battery. He found out you had taken the horse to Ander at Wyoming, and he telephoned there and Ander's father told him you were taking Quaker on to California. Father was afraid you wouldn't have money enough to get you through. He even tried to have the road police stop you so he could wire you some funds."

"Well, I'll be a badger!" Johnny said. "The mystery is solved. We thought it was the owner of Quaker, and we skulked around like fugitives from justice."

Cynthia spoke up from the bed; Miss Opal had insisted that she looked tuckered out and had propped her up there with pillows behind her back. "I thought it was *my* father. I thought he'd found out that I was on the way to California when I told him I was going to visit friends in Laramie. That's another reason I wanted to get the trunk for Miss Opal today. I was afraid he might catch up with me, somehow."

Beany thought, Then the truck driver was right. But the road police were out to help us. We needn't have dodged them; we needn't have got lost and spent that worrying night in a mountain cabin.

She addressed a card to Martie Malone on Barberry Street. Johnny cautioned her, "Don't tell him we had a rough crossing."

She wrote, "Had a wonderful trip out." Well, that wasn't stretching it too far. It had been a wonderful trip in spite of car trouble, hunger trouble, horse trouble—and heart trouble. Certainly it would be more unforgettable than if, like Mary Fred's dentist, they had clipped it off in an easy two days.

Johnny said, "We'll be laughing about that trip of ours when we're aged and gray, Maggie."

"I know," Elizabeth put in. "Don and I always say that the troubles of today are something to chuckle about for a lot of tomorrows."

Beany added to the card, "I'm glad I took the trip. . . ." What was it her father had said? "Any trip is wasted, unless you come home a little different and a little bigger person than when you started. . . ."

Beany Malone would. For one thing she had learned not to be afraid of a horse and to regard it as a hostile twelve hundred pounds of hide, teeth, and hoofs. Not that she would ever be the horsewoman Mary Fred was. But she would always remember Quaker and his grateful, even understanding, nuzzling of her when she wearily held a warm, soaked towel to his bruise.

And you couldn't be around a person like Miss Opal

without trying to live up to her faith in you. You couldn't help but put more faith in human kind. From now on, Beany vowed, I'll look for *good* in everyone.

Miss Opal had made a veritable network of friends along the way. Going back would be fun. They would be sure of a warm welcome from Della, Stella, or Bella at the Elite Café; from Mattie Leavitt, who was holding the tomato plant—and the hidden bracelet; and from Burt and Ander's folks at the Erhart ranch.

She asked, "Will Father be home when we go back, Elizabeth?"

"Yes, he'll be there waiting."

Beany's thoughts followed their Dodge on from the Erhart ranch until it turned into their driveway on Barberry Street. She warmed in anticipation of Father's greeting. She could even feel Mike's ecstatic leaps upon her, could hear Red whimper his delight. Miss Opal had told her, "It's a sweet home to come back to."

Beany spoke up suddenly to all of them, "I've been thinking about the thirty-eight dollars that I put in the trailer and Ander paid back. Maybe we'll use part of it for the return trip, though Johnny doesn't think it'll cost so much because we can make better time without the horse trailer. I was going to buy a beach outfit with my money—but—"

"What's the matter with that yellow one you got?" Norbett demanded.

"I was just thinking," Beany went on, "that I'd save it for finishing the lawn furniture at home." For she could picture that array of lawn furniture, huddled like lost, forgotten sheep under the dusty tarp under the horse chestnut tree at home, waiting for Beany.

"I should think you'd get more fun out of the lawn furniture in the long run," Cynthia proffered.

"Sure," Johnny agreed, "the summer is yet young. We can have supper outdoors and those beans by Beany cooked in a hole in the ground." He added irrelevantly, "This is Beany's vacation."

Beany looked at Norbett, at all of them in the room and her laugh bubbled over. Half of Beany's vacation was gone. It was almost time to turn around and go home.

But when Norbett said, "I'll trail along back with you. I'll relieve you of some of your load, Johnny, by taking Beany in with me," she had the wondrous feeling that her holiday was just starting.

Never had a road beckoned so hard to anyone as the road back beckoned to Beany Malone.